"DANCE WITH ME," ALEX SAID, DANGEROUSLY compelling in his pirate costume.

Katherine stepped back at the intensity in his dark eyes. "I don't think—"

He pulled her into his arms. "I've been looking for you."

Her heart jumped. I've been here all night long," she said softly.

"But not close enough." His fingers sifted through her hair, and for an instant she imagined his hands all over her body. He brushed her hair behind her bare shoulder, his gaze on her skin. The way he looked at her, she could almost believe he found her beautiful. The notion was so tantalizing that she shivered.

He drew her closer and lowered his mouth to her ear. "You told me I need to learn how to have fun." His voice was deep and rich with promise. "I want you to teach me. . . ."

WHAT ARE *LOVESWEPT* ROMANCES?

They are stories of true romance and touching emotion. We believe those two very important ingredients are constants in our highly sensual and very believable stories in the LOVESWEPT line. Our goal is to give you, the reader, stories of consistently high quality that may sometimes make you laugh, sometimes make you cry, but are always fresh and creative and contain many delightful surprises within their pages.

Most romance fans read an enormous number of books. Those they truly love, they keep. Others may be traded with friends and soon forgotten. We hope that each LOVESWEPT romance will be a treasure—a "keeper." We will always try to publish

LOVE STORIES YOU'LL NEVER FORGET
BY AUTHORS YOU'LL ALWAYS REMEMBER

The Editors

Loveswept® 641

HIS ROYAL PLEASURE

LEANNE BANKS

BANTAM BOOKS

NEW YORK · TORONTO · LONDON · SYDNEY · AUCKLAND

HIS ROYAL PLEASURE
A Bantam Book / September 1993

Thanks to Nita Taublib for "fixing the music box," and to Courtney Henke for the tinnitus.

This one is for all the grown-up little girls who ever dreamed of princes and happy endings.

ONE

"He smells."

Katherine Kendall wrinkled her nose and turned her head, wishing she could magically cause the man sprawled on her couch to disappear.

"Not that bad," Chad replied as he closed his eyes and slunk farther into the La-Z-Boy lounger.

"He smells like he took a bath in a tub of whiskey," she corrected, none too happy with being awakened at two in the morning to deal with another of Chad's misadventures.

"Well, you would, too, if someone broke a bottle of whiskey over your head." Chad warily propped open one eye, then shut it again.

Katherine tightened the belt of her kimono-style robe and planted her hands on her hips. "This is crazy. Do you even know this guy's name? He could be a mass murderer for all we know."

Grudgingly Chad opened both eyes. "All I know is he got the bottle that was aimed at my head before all hell broke loose at Chuck's Bar. Some guy punched him, and I figured the least I could do was drag him out of there and give him a place to rest for the night. He would have ended up in jail if I hadn't taken him with me."

There was a strange logic to Chad's explanation. That was frightening. When her nineteen-year-old half-brother started to make sense she was in trouble. "I've got to be up at six. Make sure Prince Charming is out of here by then. I'm going to bed."

She turned toward her bedroom.

"But you can't."

"Can't?" Katherine turned back around and arched an eyebrow.

Chad stood and gestured awkwardly toward the man on the sofa. "Somebody's gotta check him out and make sure he's okay."

"Call a doctor."

"Katie!"

"What?"

"Can't you at least look him over? I mean, you're the one who's taken first aid."

"Why didn't you take him to the clinic?"

"I didn't think he was hurt that bad. I just knew we had to get out of Chuck's."

"Is he drunk or does he have a concussion?"

Chad gave a grimace of uncertainty and shrugged.

Katherine sighed in resignation and moved toward the sofa. "Get me a damp washcloth and the first-aid kit. It's in the bathroom."

Then, as Chad prudently followed her instructions, Katherine reluctantly turned her attention to the unconscious man. He was tall, longer than the six-foot plaid sofa. His face was damp from the storm raging outside, his dark hair drenched. She gently touched his head, checking for bumps. She found one the size of a goose egg and winced. The blow must have been painful.

"So, what do you think?" Chad asked as he handed her the washcloth.

With great care Katherine sponged the man's face, neck, and head. Her instincts told her the man would be all right, and she told Chad so. Then looking at the stranger's face for the first time, she felt a vague sense of the familiar. "He looks like—" She stopped, because she couldn't put her finger on it.

"He looks like who?" Chad asked.

She squinted her eyes together and tried to concentrate. There was something about him, something that made her pulse run faster. She should know him. She searched her memory but came up with nothing.

Katherine shrugged, dismissing the odd feeling. "He looks like a mess." She studied the way his facial structure was sculpted with clean lines, high cheekbones, dark eyebrows, an aquiline nose, and a firm but compelling mouth. Uncompromising. Men would feel threatened by the arrogance in that face. Women would stare at him and make silent, secret wishes.

Other women, she thought. She would never indulge in such futile wishes. His lovers would be tall, cool, sophisticated blondes. Not, she concluded wryly, short, emotional redheads with perms from hell.

She unbuttoned his fine cotton shirt and frowned. "This doesn't fit Chuck's dress code. Have you ever met this guy before?"

"Nah, the first time I saw him was when I ducked Randy's bottle." Chad cleared his throat. "I was busy playing cards before that."

Katherine glanced knowingly at her brother. "I'll just bet you were. Did this fight have anything to do with your tendency to cheat?"

Chad shifted his feet. "Cheating's a harsh term."

Katherine closed her eyes, silently praying for restraint. Then she looked at the stranger interrupting her sleep and felt a twinge of concern.

She tried to keep her touch clinical as she pulled the wet garment from his shoulders, but Katherine was a tactile person. She liked the slide of silk against her body, the texture of well-worn cotton, and satin that caressed like warm water. She enjoyed feeling the vibration of a cat's purr, couldn't keep her hands off the peach fuzz of a baby's head, and she had a weakness for touching beautiful things.

His chest was a work of beauty—muscular, with brown male nipples peaked in protest to his cool body temperature, and a spray of dark hair that had her fingers tingling with the instinct to touch. He had biceps that inspired the thought that he was strong enough to hold a woman and keep her safe from the world.

Katherine wondered what it would be like to feel those arms around her. Instantly embarrassment surged through her. She took a deep breath.

"Can you find a robe for him? His clothes are a mess."

"Mine won't fit. He's a good four inches taller than I am," Chad pointed out.

"Look in Uncle Jasper's closet."

Checking for broken ribs, she gently ran her hands down his torso. His smooth skin warmed beneath her fingers while his chest rose and fell in the slow rhythm of peaceful sleep. His heartbeat vibrated against her palm, and she became more aware of her own pulse. It was as if there was an invisible connection between them, as if he knew her, and she knew him.

Katherine caught herself and rolled her eyes. Her lack of sleep was affecting her brain.

She needed to finish this, and the ruined trousers had to come off, she realized. After unbuckling the fine leather belt, she eased the zipper down two inches and paused. His stomach was taut and richly tan like the rest of him. She bit her lip. She'd uncovered his navel and the beginnings of dark hair on his lower abdomen.

Get on with it, silly, she thought. She clenched her jaw and pushed the zipper halfway down over his impressive masculinity and stopped abruptly. Her fingers grazed the most sensitive pleasurable part of him. Her hands were almost as close as a lover's would be.

She jerked her shaking hands away. She just couldn't do it. It was all in her mind. Nurses, doctors, and rescue workers did this kind of thing all the time. They didn't ogle. They just stripped people naked with no regard to privacy. It was their job. But Katherine couldn't get past the intimacy of the situation. Her inappropriate thoughts made her feel like an intruder, a voyeur. She'd just have to let Chad finish undressing him.

"I found one of Jasper's." Chad held the robe out to her.

"Good. I'll let you get his pants off and cover him with a blanket," she said quickly. "We can leave the robe on the back of the sofa just in case he gets up later. Then I can finish checking his head." I might want to get mine checked too, she thought.

Chad completed the job with a few groans and grunts. Katherine knelt near the man's head and applied antiseptic to the wound. It must have stung, because he moaned. The sound tore at her. "It's okay," she murmured, stroking his forehead.

Alex lifted a hand toward his head. The pain was so incredible he was tempted to go back to sleep. But his bed suddenly seemed too short, and his head felt as though an explosion had gone off inside it. Then he heard a soft, feminine voice, felt cool, gentle hands, and smelled something sweet and sultry.

"I don't think it needs stitches," the female voice said. She talked with a lazy American drawl he couldn't place. He struggled against the weight on his eyelids and willed them open.

She was blurry. He squinted his eyes, and the picture cleared. Wild auburn hair framed a solemn, cameo-featured face. Her expression was guileless and sincere. He recognized both qualities because they were so rare in his world. Her large gray eyes were wide with concern. For him? Yes, he decided, and the notion wrapped around him like a blanket.

Her skin was pale, almost alabaster perfect, except for the faint violet shadows beneath her eyes. And the sprinkling of freckles on her small nose.

"Freckles," he muttered, wondering why he couldn't recall her name.

Her pink mouth stretched into a sweet, sexy grin. "You must be okay if you can identify freckles."

Alex wondered if she were a figment of his imagination. She looked real, smelled like temptation, and had a voice that conjured up visions of lazy, hot afternoons spent in bed. He lifted his hand to her chin and watched her freeze. Her skin was silky smooth. And her lips, he thought, rubbing his thumb against them, were like rose petals. He frowned. "Why don't I remember making love to you?"

Her eyes widened, and her face bloomed with color. "Because you haven't," she whispered.

Frowning again, he dropped his hand from her mouth. What a disappointment. He'd like to think something pleasurable had precipitated this horrendous headache. None of this made sense. Why was this woman in his bed? And why had his bed shrunk? He vaguely identified the pungent smell surrounding him. "Whiskey. Not Chenin Blanc." Not the fine liquor to which he was accustomed.

Her large eyes blinked, and she cleared her throat. "Definitely not Chenin Blanc."

The soft, unmistakable weight of feminine breasts pressed pleasantly against his arm. Who was she? The throb in his head increased, and he took a deep breath to fight it. He refused to close his eyes. He didn't want to lose sight of her.

Her fine eyebrows drew together in a frown. "Get him a glass of water, Chad, please. Maybe he can take aspirin."

He heard a low murmur of response but still kept his eyes on her. "Who are you?"

She brushed her hand soothingly over his forehead. "I'm Katherine, and you're going to be okay. Here. Take some aspirin."

He took the pills and almost blacked out from the pain when she propped his head to take a drink of water. The process exhausted him. He finally closed his eyes, wondering why he hadn't made love to her.

"I think he's gone back to sleep now," Katherine said. His eyes were almost black, as dark as his hair. In those fleeting moments his dark searching gaze had had a profound effect on her; as if he'd been looking for an anchor and decided she was it.

Katherine shook her head. No way. She had an entire month and a half left to manage her uncle's resort. Her time and attention were spoken for.

"You think he'll be okay?" Chad looked guilty.

Katherine's heart softened toward her brother. He was at a tough stage in life: not quite man, not quite boy. The fact that their mother had just entered the blissful state of matrimony for the fifth time didn't exactly help matters.

Katherine was convinced that underneath—*way underneath*—all his selfishness lay a heart of gold. She squeezed his arm. "He'll be fine. And I think you did the right thing by bringing him here." She paused, thinking of how her heart had tripped when the handsome stranger wrapped her in his warm gaze. There was something familiar, yet forbidden, about him.

She squared her shoulders. "But I want him out of here by tomorrow afternoon."

When Alex awoke the next morning, he couldn't decide which was worse: the crick in his neck or the teeth-clenching pain in his head. He looked around the unfamiliar room and felt confused. Then the events of the previous evening came back to him. Katherine and the young man named Chad. He hadn't seen the bottle coming until it was too late. The wet trip over on the ferry. He rose stiffly.

Chad entered from another room. "So, how's the head?"

Alex quirked his mouth. "In the future I'll always associate the smell of cheap whiskey with pain."

Chad grinned and offered a cup of coffee. "You and the rest of the world."

He accepted it and took a drink. It was weaker than what he was accustomed to. "Thank you."

"No. Thank *you*. I'm sorry about the bottle last night." Chad shrugged his shoulders. "If there's anything I can do . . ."

He glanced down at his bare chest and legs. "A shower and some clothes?"

Chad seemed glad to have something to do. "Sure. There's a mechanic who takes care of the rides who's about your size." He headed for the front door. "And the bathroom is the second door on your right."

"Chad," Alex called. "Where am I?"

"Nowhere."

Alex frowned.

"Well," Chad amended quickly, "specifically, you're on Pirate Island, population four hundred sixty-four on a busy day. This is a camping resort for families who want to get away from it all. And I say 'all' in the literal sense. We don't even have a weekly newspaper, and the only way you can get here is by ferry." Chad hooked his fingers in his pockets and leaned forward conspiratorially. "Elvis could live here in total obscurity. The place is dead."

Alex was sure he'd misunderstood. "No newspaper?"

"None."

"Radio or television station?"

"None." Chad pushed open the door. "Don't worry. We won't keep you here. The noon ferry will be here before you know it."

Alex stared after Chad thoughtfully. No newspaper. No media. No "Your Majesty." An insane idea struck him. He immediately dismissed it. But as he took his shower and ate a bowl of cereal, it distracted him like a buzzing bee.

He called the palace collect and asked for Isabella. Though Alex felt distant from his three siblings, he felt the strongest connection with Isabella, probably because she was the closest in age and she didn't stand on ceremony with him.

"Where are you?" she asked without preamble. "Jake called this morning and said you hadn't arrived."

"You haven't mentioned this to Father."

"No, but I would have if you hadn't called in another hour. Jake asked where you were, then he rudely ordered me to keep my mouth shut. Your friend is—"

"—Jake's an American, and he was right to ask you to keep quiet."

"He didn't ask," she stiffly informed him.

Alex shook his head. This would have been easier if he could have talked to his longtime assistant, Max, but Max was in Tibet. "That's beside the point. I'm on Pirate Island, North Carolina. I had some—" he paused only a second—"transportation difficulties. It's a remote area. No media. They don't even know who I am."

"Sounds enthralling. When are you going to Jake's?"

"I don't know." He looked around the simply furnished room and finally repeated his impulse out loud. "I was thinking of staying."

Complete silence followed his statement, which was rare for Isabella. "You're joking," she finally said. "You wouldn't last a week without your adoring servants."

That nettled him. "I've handled tougher conditions than this."

"But everybody always knew you were Prince Alexander Ferdinand Merrick de Moreno."

True. That was what he loved and hated about Isabella—she always told the truth.

"Alex, face it. You're a prince. When you take the throne, you'll be a king. You're good at being a ruler. It's your identity."

Familiar dissatisfaction rolled through him. He loved his country and took seriously his role as leader, but even leaders needed an occasional break. That was the purpose behind this monthlong vacation. A dozen practical objections to his staying on Pirate Island came to mind.

The once-in-a-lifetime opportunity to be just a man, though, won out. In that instant he made his decision. "Call Jake and give my regrets. He'll understand. Have the rental car picked up in Charles City. I'll see you in a month."

"I don't believe this. You'll never last."

Alex knew Isabella couldn't resist a bet. "Shall we wager?"

"What?"

"If I don't last a month, I'll persuade Father to let you go to Monte Carlo with your wild friend Lucinda."

"She's not that wild," Isabella corrected.

"If I stay, you make the same kind of trip—sans title." While Alex wore his title like a cloak, Isabella used hers as a shield to get out of sticky situations.

"Deal."

"Not a word to Mother or Father."

"My lips are sealed. I'll be too busy thinking about Monte Carlo."

Alex smiled. "Just remember my nickname, dearest."

"Prince of Steel? Ah, but even steel melts, Your High and Mightiness." She paused, and her voice softened. "Take care. *Au revoir*, Alex."

"Make that Al. Al Sanders."

"*Au revoir*." She hesitated. "Al."

Twenty minutes later his new identity was firmly in place. From the tight fit of the borrowed jeans and T-shirt brought to him, Alex concluded the mechanic weighed about twenty pounds less than he did. He learned that Chad and Katherine's uncle Jasper owned the campground but had recently experienced a heart attack. Katherine was nearly overwhelmed with the responsibility of the busy tourist season.

He also learned despite Chad's stuttering and stammering that Katherine expected Alex to vacate the premises as soon as possible.

Alex, however, had other ideas. He wanted to take advantage of the opportunity to be a nonprince.

After all, it might never come again. He needed to be just a man. Katherine needed help. The solution seemed simple to him. And in the back of his mind, he wanted to learn more about the tough and tender lady with the rose-petal mouth.

Alex picked up a map of the resort complex and set out to make himself indispensable.

At nine o'clock that evening Katherine glanced up to find Al Sanders propped against the door of her uncle's office. He should have been gone hours ago. Instead, he'd entertained some difficult customers by taking them sailing. The disgruntled couple had been charmed, the woman nearly melting into the cracks of the pavement.

Katherine couldn't blame her. When Al looked into a woman's eyes as though she were the only female in the world, he dissolved defenses more effectively than the Patriot missile. And those breathtakingly tight jeans could surely earn him a spot in the buns-of-steel calendar. Add in his hundred-dollar smile and masterful air, and Katherine was surprised women hadn't started throwing their lingerie at him.

She was pretty sure Al Sanders was a con artist down on his luck, and she wanted him gone before he caused any trouble. The fact that he unsettled her and she couldn't put her finger on why only added fuel to the fire.

It would have been much easier to kick his incredible derriere off the island if he hadn't sold helium balloons and skipped dinner to sell cotton candy, she realized.

Remembering his injured head, she felt guilty. She motioned for him to sit and offered him some packaged bologna sandwiches and a soda. Maybe if she fed him, she wouldn't feel so bad about sending him off.

"How's your head?"

"Fine."

But he looked a little green. She set some aspirin in front of him.

"Thank you."

Katherine took a deep breath and sat in her uncle's worn captain's chair behind the old walnut desk. Her least favorite thing in the world was firing people. And although technically, she'd never hired Al, the process was still the same. Her palms were sweating.

She thought of how her uncle would handle this situation, pretended she was six feet tall instead of five foot three, and tried to forget that she was much more comfortable teaching first graders than managing this camping resort.

"Al, I appreciate how you've pitched in today.

And I'll be glad to pay you for your services," she began, and twined her fingers together.

"That's unnecessary. I wanted to thank you for your kindness last night." Al glanced down at the sandwich. "This meat is unusual. It's very good."

Katherine blinked. "It's bologna."

He looked thoughtful. "I'll have to remember that."

She narrowed her eyes. "You have an accent. Are you from England?"

"I've spent some time there."

"Do you have a green card?" she asked, hoping for an easy out.

He stiffened. "I don't need a green card."

His manner was so cold and affronted, she had to resist the urge to apologize. Such pride, she thought. It was surpassed only by his confidence. She'd always resented tall, confident people.

Katherine tried the direct approach. "The next ferry leaves at ten o'clock. We're booked for the night, but there are some nice hotels on the mainland."

"You have a room available in your cabin. Chad tells me you're short-staffed and this is the busy season. I'd like to work for room and board until the end of the month."

Katherine mentally cursed her half-brother and picked up a pencil. "Al, you arrived here last night, drunk and passed out. I don't really see how I can hire you on that basis."

"I arrived here passed out because I happened into a bottle of whiskey aimed for your brother's head. I was not drunk."

He stood and dropped the paper napkin into the trash. Then he looked directly at her. "Have you been unhappy with my performance today?"

Katherine leaned back in her chair. "Well, no."

"Are you short-staffed?"

She resisted the urge to squirm. "Yes."

He shrugged his broad shoulders. "Take me on a trial basis."

Her chest squeezed tight. What woman wouldn't take him? He was the kind of man women made fools of themselves over. If she had erotic dreams, he would be the kind of lover she'd dream of. His hands would be slow and sure, his mouth both giving and ruthless, his voice low and urgent. She shivered.

"Trial basis," she repeated weakly.

"Yes." He glanced away from her, suddenly appearing tired. "I'm rather . . ."

". . . down on your luck at the moment," she supplied for him.

His dark eyes held wry, weary amusement. "So, you're not only beautiful, you're also perceptive." He bent over the desk and took her fidgeting hand. "What have you got to lose?"

Katherine's cheeks heated at the feeling of her hand enveloped within his larger one. *Beautiful?* Lord, he's good, she thought. She pulled her hand away and cleared her throat.

She couldn't say what tipped the scales in his favor. Maybe it was the fact that he'd worked so hard this afternoon. It might have been that she wondered if she'd misjudged him. What if he wasn't a con man and needed help? Katherine was sensitive to unfairness, having taken too many cheap shots from the tabloids over her ex-husband's affairs.

But what really affected her was the way his posture screamed confidence while his eyes revealed flashes of something deeper and more human.

"One week's trial," she finally said, and watched him relax slightly.

"You won't regret it."

Katherine gave a grim smile and prayed.

Katherine awoke to darkness and the sound of someone scratching on her window screen. After a moment of terror she recognized old Mr. Larson's husky voice. He wanted to borrow fishing lures from her uncle and had forgotten Jasper was gone for the summer. Katherine promised to find them, and Mr. Larson said he'd be back in twenty minutes.

Pushing her hair from her face, she crept from her room to the hall closet. She shined the flashlight up the shelves to the top one and sighed. There sat the tackle box.

She tiptoed to the kitchen and grabbed a barstool. After positioning it in front of the closet, she climbed on top and reached for the box.

"What are you doing?" a low voice said behind her.

Startled, Katherine gave a muffled squeak. The barstool shifted. She panicked until the stool was steadied and a strong arm wrapped around her waist.

She took deep breaths to calm her racing heart. "What are you doing?" she whispered.

"That's what I asked you," Al said. "Do you know what time it is?"

"No. And please don't tell me. I've got to get fishing lures for Mr. Larson. He and Uncle Jasper always go fishing together this time of year." She moaned. "They'd leave about four o'clock in the morning."

"You're close. It's actually—"

"I said don't tell me."

His chuckle rumbled pleasantly out of the darkness. His arm felt warm around her. She'd rested her hand on it and could feel his flexed muscles. Her back absorbed the sensation of his hard chest pressed against her. His musky male scent made her lightheaded. The darkness covered them like a blanket, and their hushed voices made the situation feel oddly erotic.

"Let me go."

"No. You might fall."

She started to argue, then realized it would be faster just to grab the tackle box and get down. She turned around with the tackle box in her hand. Al took it, and before she could bend down, he picked her up. She clutched his shoulders and slid down his body, feeling his bare chest against her breasts. Her hair shimmied over one of his shoulders.

She looked into his face, and everything stopped. Her mind, her heart, her breath. Somewhere in her conscience the hint of a melody, stirring and poignant, teased her. At that moment all she could do was stand still inside his arms and watch.

With one arm still wrapped around her waist, he picked up the long lock of hair and rubbed it between his fingers. "It's so long," he mused.

Katherine's mouth went dry. "I—I keep saying I'm going to cut it."

"No, it's you. Long red hair, slim little body, lots of warm smiles."

She sucked in a deep, desperate breath. Laughing nervously, she tried to step back. "How do you know anything about me? You just met me."

He released her slowly, and she could make out the intent look in his eyes even in the darkness. "You learn by watching and listening. I've done both."

"Oh," she said. She shook back the distracting hair, relieved to be out of his arms.

"Why are you managing this place on your own?" he asked.

"My uncle had a heart attack. I'm the only one he trusts."

"But you don't like it."

That stopped her. "Does it show that much?" She sighed. "I teach first grade during the school year and head up the children's programs for Pirate Island during the summer. Jasper's heart attack caught all of us by surprise." She shrugged. "I may not be a wonderful manager, but I think with a little help I can hold things together until he decides what he wants to do."

"It's a heavy responsibility."

"Yeah." Katherine grinned and picked up the tackle box. "But I'm tough."

He put his hand on hers. "Let me take that."

"I can handle it," she insisted.

"I'm sure you can."

Katherine stared at him to see if he was making fun of her. But his gaze was serious. "Okay. Just put it on the front porch, please."

She set the barstool back in the kitchen. "See ya in the morning," she whispered.

"That will be in about two hours," Al said.

Katherine moaned. "Don't rub it in."

After she closed her door and settled into bed, Katherine stared at the ceiling. She wasn't sure about Al Sanders. Too many things didn't add up.

Who was he? Why was he staying on Pirate Island? Why did she care? She wrestled with the questions until she finally fell asleep.

Then she dreamed she danced in the dark. She couldn't quite make out the face of her partner, but his shoulders were broad, his arms strong, and the music she heard touched a tender, vulnerable place inside her.

TWO

Katherine hung up the phone and stared at it. She felt as if she'd just committed a murder.

It was the right thing to do, she told herself. After all, this was Jasper's third heart attack. The doctor had warned Jasper to cut back on his level of responsibility. Even though her uncle wouldn't admit it, he had no business managing the campground any longer. By putting the word out that they were interested in selling, she was just making it easier for him. Ultimately the final decision would be Jasper's. But Katherine reasoned that if she took care of the legwork, selling the campground wouldn't be so traumatic for him.

Then why did she feel so horrible? It was probably because Uncle Jasper and Pirate Island were the two most stable elements in her life. Since Katherine had turned six, she'd spent every summer with Jasper at the campground. On high school breaks she'd led the children's programs.

Between her mother's ventures in and out of matrimony and the corresponding upheavals in all their lives, Katherine had clung to Pirate Island as if it were a lifeline. Now, she was cutting it.

The thought made her sick.

From her disappointing relationship with her father to her publicly humiliating divorce, Katherine's luck with men had been the pits. The only exception was Uncle Jasper, who'd taught her to fish, encouraged her to go to college, and taught her the value of honesty and stability.

She sighed, wishing there was another way.

"Bad news?" Al asked from behind her.

He moved closer, watching her turn away and give her cheek a surreptitious wipe. "Why didn't you knock?"

"I did. You must not have heard me." Alex hesitated, wondering what to do. He'd dealt with teary females before, but in his experience, women usually cried in order to get something. Specifically they cried when they found out he wasn't going to marry them, and they weren't going to be the next princess of Moreno.

Katherine, however, appeared genuinely upset, and that bothered him. "You're upset. What do you need?"

She shook her head and forced a cheerful expression on her face. "Nothing. It's nothing."

Alex narrowed his eyes. "If it's nothing, then why is your lip quivering?" He reached a hand to her face.

"You're very observant," she murmured, moving to the other end of the small office.

"Yes. You didn't answer my question."

She made a sound that was half exasperation and half laughter. "You're also pushy."

"Persistent," he corrected. "What's wrong?"

Katherine rolled her eyes. "It's none of your business."

He frowned. No one had ever said that to him. Not his mother, not even Isabella. Katherine Kendall was an irritating feminine puzzle. She'd reluctantly taken him in but kept her distance during the last week. And though she didn't trust him, she was beginning to rely on him. He was making damn sure of that.

He was curious about her. The way the campground children followed her around as if she were the Pied Piper. She gave smiles away for free, hugs as if they were pennies.

To everyone but him.

He minded being excluded from her smiles, hugs, and everything else. He noticed the way she used her petite body carelessly, as if she thought there was nothing sensual about the way she walked, but he sensed something simmering beneath the surface. Her slim waist and full breasts made him want to wrap his hands around her, touch her silky skin, learn her secrets. When she talked, sometimes he got hard just watching her mouth.

And if she knew what he was thinking, he'd be on the next ferry out of here. For the first time in his life Alex wanted something he'd never wanted from a woman. If only for the remainder of this month, he wanted possession of the mind, body, and soul of Katherine. His obstacle was that the lady didn't trust him.

Patience had never been his long suit. He moved forward. Katherine took a matching step away. He stopped. "Why do you do that?" he asked.

She curled her hands around the edge of the desk. "Do what?"

"Move away as if you're afraid I'll attack you."

Her eyes opened wide. "Do I do that? I, uh, I didn't realize." She pushed back her bangs and jammed her hand into the pocket of her pink cotton shorts.

"Are you afraid of me?"

"No! Of course not," she said quickly, but the silence stretched between them.

"No?"

Katherine sighed, then said reluctantly, "This is embarrassing. I don't know you, but I feel like I should. You remind me of someone, but I can't remember who."

For a second he froze, wondering if she'd seen a publicity photo of him. He forced a casual shrug. "Someone you knew when you were young?"

"No," she admitted.

Alex wondered at the sudden color in her cheeks. "Is it my face?"

She looked trapped. "Yes, your face and your ..."

"My what?"

"Your eyes."

"And?"

Maybe if she said it out loud, the strange feeling would go away. "And your body. It's ridiculous. I know. It's insane, but I have this feeling that I've known you . . ." She lifted her hands, searching for the word she couldn't bring herself to say. And there was no way on God's green earth she'd tell him about the music.

Alex smiled. "Intimately."

"But we both know it's not possible," she went on quickly, not liking the satisfaction she heard in his voice. "I've never met you. You've never met me. It's just—"

He touched her, and her mile-a-minute denial cut off. Her vocal cords jammed. He cupped her chin, gently encouraging her to meet his gaze, and Katherine knew she was in major-league trouble.

"If I had met you, *mon amie*, I couldn't have forgotten. Perhaps we met in another life."

"I, uh, I don't really believe in reincarnation," she managed breathlessly.

"Neither do I." His face grew serious. "But there are other ways—dreams, fantasies."

Katherine squished her eyes shut, fighting his words and the images he provoked. "I don't have a lot of time for dreams or fantasies."

"Fantasies make time for themselves."

He wrapped his warm hand around her waist, and she thought she'd faint. Oh, God, she didn't want to make a fool of herself. She'd done such a good job of it before. She clenched her jaw.

"I dreamed of you," he said. "I dreamed I tasted your smile. I made love to your mouth for a day and a night, because I couldn't stop. Then I brought you so close, there was nothing between us."

Keeping her eyes closed, she felt him lower his head, felt his warm breath, got dizzy over his heat and strength. The melody began again, so sweetly it hurt. She waited, dreaded, wished.

His mouth barely whispered against hers in an openly erotic touch that coaxed and threatened and sent her pulse into triple time. She saw herself falling down deep into a well that never ended. No safety net. No coming back.

It scared her spitless. Katherine jerked back, her eyes flying open. "No!"

"No?" he repeated, as if he were unfamiliar with the meaning of the word.

"N-o-o." She drew it out so he wouldn't miss it, and she was beginning to think she needed some practice with that word herself. She was going to need ice for the burn marks where he'd touched her. "This weird feeling will go away," she insisted. "It's not real, and we don't need to act on it."

"Not real."

Her insides still felt like a five-alarm fire. "Exactly. It's good that we both understand. It's perfectly clear." Clear as mud, she thought. Without a hint of conversational finesse, she forced the conversation back to business. "Is there a problem somewhere on the campground? Or did you have a question?"

He paused, studying her, and she knew she hadn't fooled him. Such dark, perceptive eyes Al Sanders had. She waited out the uncomfortable silence, hoping he'd relent.

"Do you know anything about a balloon battle?" he finally asked.

Katherine laughed in relief and nodded at his quizzical expression. "Yes." She checked her watch. "Oops, we'd better hurry or we'll be late. Wednesdays at two o'clock sharp, all the kids and some adults engage in a water-balloon battle."

Grateful for something to break the spell, she

grabbed some bags of balloons from a drawer and led the way out of the office.

"A game," Al concluded.

"Sort of."

"And what is the objective?"

Katherine came to a stop on the wooden front porch of the rec building and looked at him. "You've never been in a water-balloon battle?" When he shook his head, she made a tsk-ing sound. "The objective of a water-balloon battle is to get everyone wet and to laugh a lot."

"But who wins?"

"No one."

"Then why?"

"For fun," she said, wondering why the concept seemed foreign to him. "Like making mud pies when you were three."

Alex looked at her blankly. Mud pies?

"Seeing who can do the worst belly flopper off the side of the pool?"

His German swimming instructor had allowed only perfect dives. He shook his head.

Katherine was determined to find common ground. "Who can blow the biggest bubble-gum bubble?"

Alex's lips twitched at that. He could just imagine the appalled expression on his etiquette instructor's face if the future ruler of Moreno had suggested a bubble-blowing contest. "Try again."

"Okay. Last one. Little boys are famous for this. Who can spit the farthest?"

He laughed out loud. "You're joking."

Katherine smiled, liking the rare sound of his deep chuckle. "No. And if you've never done any of those things, you're either an alien or you were raised in a bubble."

He felt his grin fall, remembering the scandal that had rocked his childhood. "You could be right."

The turbulence in his dark eyes tugged at her. Al obviously knew how to have the adult brand of fun. He was an expert at everything from sailing and charming conversation to seducing a woman. But he seemed lost when it came to carefree, silly, child-like fun. It made her wonder what he'd missed. It made her care. She deliberately kept her tone light. "An extraterrestrial. The kids'll love it. Well, get ready for a new experience."

About thirty kids, some of them over thirty years old, stood in the grassy area set aside for outside recreational games. They wore bathing suits and were screaming for blood.

In between filling the balloons with water, Chad was inciting the crowd to all kinds of watery violence. When they saw Katherine with more balloons, they cheered. Katherine and Al filled the rest of the balloons while Chad divided the group into teams.

"That should be enough," Katherine said, and began to put the balloons into two separate piles. "If you don't want to play, you'd better—"

Splat.

Alex jumped as the balloon burst against his back, cold water seeping into his shirt and pants. He looked over his shoulder at the culprit, a pigtailed little girl. He was so shocked, it must have shown on his face. Her eyes grew huge with fright, and she began to run away.

"Stacy!" Katherine caught her and handed the little girl another balloon. Uncertain, Stacy looked from Katherine to Alex. Katherine gave her a nudge of encouragement, and little Stacy heaved the balloon smack into the side of his head.

Alex took it like a man. With water dripping off his nose and eyelashes, he even managed a smile for the little feminine warrior. "This is fun?" he asked Katherine when Stacy ran off yelling in victory. "Am I supposed to thank you?"

Katherine didn't bother hiding her laughter. "Well, I bet you're cooler now."

There was another *splat*. Katherine shrieked, snatched up a balloon from the rapidly depleting supply, and threw it at her attacker.

Catching the spirit of the event, he took a balloon, testing its weight in his hand. Katherine turned, laughing, then shaking her head when she saw the balloon in his hand.

"No," she said, backing away.

"I owe you." Going against every rule he'd ever learned about how to treat a woman, he threw it and scored a direct hit.

"Al Sanders!" she yelled, clearly torn between laughter and indignation. "You'll pay!"

But the balloon she tossed back barely fazed him. He was too busy looking at Katherine. Her eyes were full of laughter. Her wet shirt stretched like a second skin across her breasts. Her nipples strained against the drenched cloth, begging for a man's hands and mouth, he thought, and felt a corresponding thickness in his loins. Suddenly he understood the appeal of a water-balloon battle.

Katherine sat on the beach at midnight wearing a flowing blue dress that dropped off one shoulder. She was waiting for something, somebody, as she dug her bare toes into the cool sand and lifted her head to the breeze.

She closed her eyes until something soft brushed her cheek, and the scent of a rose reached her nostrils. She looked up, and he was there.

He smiled and drew her to her feet. "Where have you been hiding?"

Her heart sped up. "I haven't been hiding. I've been waiting."

"For me," he said with customary arrogance.

"*Maybe.*"

He pulled her close. "*Who knows you like I do? Who knows what pleases you?*"

She felt a wave of uncertainty. "*Sometimes I don't even know me.*"

"*Yes, you do.*" *He rubbed his thumb over her lower lip.* "*And what you don't know, I'll teach you.*"

She shivered at the intensity in his dark eyes. What if he tried and found her lacking?

He must have read her mind. "*Never.*"

Holding her gaze, he continued to rub her lip. Hesitantly, Katherine stroked his thumb with the tip of her tongue. He tasted warm and a little salty and male. Something dipped and swayed within her at the small intimacy.

"*Good,*" *he said. He glazed his thumb over the edge of her lower teeth, and she bit down gently. She saw the approval in his eyes and felt a rush of pleasure. She'd pleased him. Then she pleased herself and suckled. The heaviness in her abdomen surprised her.*

"*You make it difficult to wait, Katherine,*" *he muttered in a strained voice. He pulled his hand away and brought hers to his mouth.* "*But turnabout is fair play, no?*"

He kissed the palm of her hand. Then he sucked a finger into his mouth. The sensation drew her nipples tight. Embarrassed, she wondered how to hide it.

"*There's no need to hide your desire,* chérie. *It pleases me.*" *He gave her finger a playful nip and placed her hand on his shoulder. Then he touched one of her nipples.*

She gasped. The gentle caress stung. She was too needy, too soon. It made her feel weak and vulnerable.

He seemed to understand. "How long have you been this way?"

"Too long," she breathed. "Much too long."

Anger flashed in his eyes, then passed. He pulled her into a comforting hug. She sighed against his white shirt. Beneath her cheek, she felt the beat of his heart, the hard, warm muscle of his chest.

"I'm not like other men. Are you ready for me, Katherine?"

She wasn't sure, but was it a matter of choice? It felt inevitable. She lifted her head. "I don't know what to tell you."

"What do you want?"

She swallowed and somehow found the courage. "I want to feel your mouth against mine. I want to taste you. I want you to taste me. I want you to want me," she whispered, realizing she'd made herself completely vulnerable.

"If it's in my power, I will always give you what you want," he said in a deep, rough voice.

He lowered his mouth, and she waited and wanted. The music began. She felt the first brush of his lips and melted. The wanting got worse.

She reached for him, but her fingers were suddenly empty. He was fading.

She panicked. "No!" she cried, but he'd turned into mist.

"Don't go."

"No!"

The dampness from her eyes woke her. Her breath backed up in her chest, and she blinked hard, staring at her ceiling. "Oh, God." She threw an arm up over her eyes. "It was just a dream."

Katherine rolled onto her side and curled into a ball. The anguish still flowed through her. It was worse than a nightmare. Her subconscious had played the most cruel of jokes on her this time. That she could please a man was impossible. God knows, she'd tried every trick in the book with her ex-husband. Making love had been the most awkward, humiliating experience of her life.

Twice now, she'd dreamed of Al and heard that damned music in the background. It was because of that kiss this afternoon. Her lips tingled even now at the memory. She touched them.

Unsettled, she kicked off the covers. She was too warm, yet goose bumps stood up on her skin. Why was this happening to her? What did it mean? She took a deep breath, fighting and accepting the crazy truth. It meant she was vulnerable to Al Sanders, and she'd best watch her step if she didn't want heart trouble.

After a busy Saturday spent checking in the new week's campers, Katherine was glad to escape for a late-night swim. She took a little extra time in the ocean, knowing she'd pay for it tomorrow morning. Finally, she reluctantly left the warm, caressing waves.

There was Al standing on the sand, next to her T-shirt. The crazy dream flashed through her mind, and her heart tightened in her chest. Willing herself to relax, she made her way to his side and reached for her balled-up T-shirt. She'd forgotten a towel again.

Al's gaze lingered on her wet, scantily clad body for a long moment, then he draped a towel over her shoulders. "I brought this for you."

His kindness made her contrite for being so guarded. "Thank you. It's a beautiful night, isn't it?"

"Yes." Al sat down and patted the sand beside him. "Join me."

Katherine paused in the act of rubbing herself dry. He'd done it again. Was that a request or an order? Then again, after midnight, who cared?

"I love the ocean," she said, watching the pulse of the whitecaps against the sand. "During the school year I live in Greensboro. So I really miss it then."

"You're going to miss it even more when Pirate Island is sold."

Katherine stiffened. "How—"

"You got a call from Mr. James Logan. He'd heard from someone in Charles City, and he wants to tour the campground with you tomorrow morning at ten o'clock."

"Tomorrow!" The news hit her like a brick. Even though she knew selling Pirate Island was for the best, taking this next step hurt. She wasn't ready emotionally or logistically.

"Oh, this is just great." She stood and struggled with her T-shirt. "We've got a ton of children's activities planned tomorrow morning. It's supposed to rain, so all the parents will be dumping their kids on us." Trying to pull the armhole of the shirt over her head, she made a muffled sound of frustration. "What is wrong with this shirt?"

"I'm sure Chad and the others will cooperate with you once you tell them your plan," Al said, deftly righting the shirt for her.

She jerked the shirt on and glared at him. "I don't want Chad and the others to know. For that matter I don't want *you* to know. But I guess it's too late for that."

"And your uncle Jasper?"

Katherine gripped his arm. "Swear you won't tell him."

"I won't. But you shouldn't have to do this alone. You care too much about this place. You can trust me."

Katherine stared at him. She almost believed him. He stood there so tall, so sure, so strong. She could feel muscles like steel beneath her fingers. She dropped her hands, but he caught them.

He was getting too close. She felt crowded. She'd always felt more comfortable helping others than being helped. Katherine tried to pull her hands away, but he wouldn't allow it. She pulled her gaze from his instead.

"Let me help you," Al said in a low murmur that sent goosebumps down her arms. "Call it payback," he offered. "You took me in when I needed help."

"I didn't want to."

"But you did."

Katherine finally succeeded in pulling away. "I don't know you."

Al shook his head. "You know me. You told me so yourself. You're not following your instincts."

Her stomach fluttered, but she held her ground. "My instincts with men haven't been very reliable."

"Then you must follow *my* instincts."

Katherine blinked and checked the hard planes of his face. He was serious. "Has anyone ever told you you're the teeniest bit autocratic?"

Alex considered that. "No. People are grateful for my advice."

"Or maybe they're just too intimidated to point out your arrogance," she muttered.

Alex was just about to firmly address her breach

of protocol when he remembered that Al Sanders wasn't due any special treatment. He stared down at the woman who got under his skin more than any other had and reined in his consternation. "I prefer to call it confidence."

"Well, I can't argue with that," she said in a dry tone.

"Are you so frightened of me?"

He watched her face and realized he'd hit a nerve. His quick surge of triumph gave way to something less comfortable. He took her hands again.

"Can't you just leave me alone?" she whispered, hoping to appeal to his mile-wide chivalrous streak.

Alex shook his head.

A lump of dread formed in her throat. The sheer power of his personality overwhelmed her. He was so sure of himself. His hands, she noticed irrelevantly, were warm and firm, just as they'd been in her dream.

He pulled her closer.

Katherine's heart raced. *Oh, no*. Not on the beach. Not when she felt weak and confused.

Not tonight.

Not any time.

THREE

It was inevitable, Katherine realized. She braced herself, stiffening her body, closing her eyes, and tightly pursing her lips. Then she waited.

For a moment nothing happened. His hands still held hers, his breath mingled with the night breeze against her cheek, and his body emanated heat and power, but he didn't move any closer to her.

Then he rubbed his lips across her cheek and chuckled next to her ear. The tickling vibration of his voice had her curling her head toward her shoulder. She opened her eyes and glared at him for laughing at her.

"You look like you're preparing yourself for a vile-tasting medicine," he said. "Am I so bad, *chérie?*"

"Very bad," Katherine shot back. When she realized how tightly she clutched his hands, she struggled to release them.

He ignored her struggles. "Ah, but how can you know when you haven't learned my flavor?"

"I don't wa—"

The rest of her words and breath were lost as his mouth came down on hers. She tried to purse her mouth again, but he sucked her lower lip and darted his tongue across her upper one.

He gave her a moment's respite, and she grabbed it as if it were a lifeline. "Cheater," she hissed, breathless and angry because of it. "You've got my hands."

In an instant he released them, but before she could do anything, Al slid his hands through her hair, cradling her head. "It's a sin to see a frown on such a beautiful mouth," he chided in a velvet tone that sent shivers down her spine.

"I'm sure you're an expert on sin."

At his soft laughter she balled her fists and thought about bopping him on his hard head. Her ability to move, however, evaporated when he nibbled, then pressed his mouth against hers first one way, then another, and another, until she grew soft beneath him.

He was sipping her like nectar. His tongue explored the tenderness just inside her lips. She felt like a rare delicacy he was savoring to the fullest. Her heart thundered against her chest, and she sighed, dropping her fists in mute surrender.

One of his hands slid down her hair to her bare

back, pressing her closer so that she felt the muscles of his chest, the tightness of his abdomen, the power of his thighs and the hard ridge between. And she knew he really wanted her. He wasn't putting on an act that would end up making her feel foolish and humiliated.

"Taste me, Katherine," he murmured. His voice was needy, irresistibly needy.

She couldn't find the reserves to fight him. Rubbing her tongue against his, she tested the texture of his teeth and the roof of his mouth. He made a gruff, masculine sound of approval.

Needing something to hold on to, she clung to his shoulders, her fingers squeezing restlessly. Her breasts were heavy, and she ached in secret places.

As he mercilessly plundered her mouth, Katherine was lost to everything but him. She felt a clench deep inside her, increasing waves of sensation that threatened to drown her with their intensity.

"Oh, my God," she moaned, tearing herself from his arms.

Utterly and completely humiliated, she wrapped her arms around herself and turned away gasping for air. For God's sake, what was wrong with her? All he'd done was kiss her.

"Katherine," he said, putting his hand on her shoulder.

She jerked away. "No! Don't touch. Don't talk. Just leave me alone." She heard the huskiness in both their voices, felt his uneven breath on her shoulder, and nearly cried.

"But you're upset."

"I'll be okay. Just give me a minute alone."

He paused. "I can't leave you like this. Not after—"

"Let's not talk about it," she said desperately. She cringed at the intimacy between them. He was too experienced not to know how aroused she'd been.

"Look at me, Katherine."

There it was again, the note of command in his voice.

When she looked up at him, his hair was ruffled by the wind, his dark eyes blazing with blunt desire. His cheeks flared with the dusky flush of passion. And as she looked at his swollen lips, she touched her own.

"You're not alone," he said.

She almost believed him. "Maybe not at this moment, but eventually I will be. It always ends that way." The breeze cooled her face and gave her strength. "I'm just an ordinary woman who will end up getting hurt." She paused, shaking her head. "I don't know much about you, Al Sanders, but I know you're not like other men."

His eyes flickered, then narrowed. The warmth of passion faded to something cold and bleak.

He's angry, she thought. He might even be hurt. The notion didn't sit well. She tried to say something but couldn't think of anything that didn't leave her too vulnerable.

Al turned away, effectively dismissing her.

Something inside her compelled her to go after him. *Don't let him be lonely.* But then she caught herself and forced herself to be still. This man could destroy her.

For several long moments Katherine watched him, her mind and heart pulling in opposite directions. Finally she turned away and walked up the beach, shivering the whole way home, wondering why she felt so empty.

The next morning Katherine focused on her upcoming appointment with James Logan. She persuaded Chad and one of her most dependable employees, Suzanne, to help out with the children. Katherine gave them a milelong list of activities to do while she met with Mr. Logan.

James Logan was a clever, middle-aged resort owner who talked circles around Katherine's sales spiel. He'd griped the entire time. She countered each of his criticisms of the campground with a positive statement.

He didn't like the layout. He didn't like the menu at lunch. He didn't like the color of the paint in the cabins. Katherine just smiled and pointed out that beige didn't show dirt.

He didn't seem to like much of anything. When they'd concluded the excruciatingly thorough tour, he'd said, "I'll call you." Translated: *You'll never hear from me again*.

Katherine was tired enough to be more relieved than disappointed. The only thing she wanted now was a six-hour bath. Her conscience chided her to check on how Suzanne and Chad were doing, so she hustled the rest of the way to the front porch. Pulling off the plastic poncho, Katherine laughed at her wet, mud-splattered appearance. "Give me a white flag," she murmured to herself.

The sound of applause filtered through the wooden door. Curious, she opened it and caught sight of Chad and a group of little boys playing cards. They were chewing gum and swilling Kool-Aid. A sliver of unease sifted through her. Chad wouldn't teach them poker, would he?

Noting the backs of the cards, Katherine relaxed. Old Maid.

She pushed the door open wider. The activity on the other side of the room stopped her midmotion. A lamp, minus its shade, perched on a low stool. A small army of boys and girls holding switches lunged and feinted as if sword fighting. Their movements created a dancing display of shadows on the far wall.

Al called out and showed them a movement. They stopped to watch, then, in unison, imitated his precision with childlike awkwardness.

"*En garde*," he said in a commander's voice.

"*En garde*," they returned, and copied his bow.

A chill ran down her spine.

The whole scene carried an air of unreality. Al feinted and parried with his imaginary opponent, moving with agility and skill. His shadow looked larger than life. She could almost imagine him in times of old, protecting, defending, conquering.

His powerful body flexed with tension. His face was set with concentration. This was no game for him, Katherine sensed. It made her wonder about him. Who was he? Why was he here? What did he want from her?

He lunged and took the killing stroke through the heart of his victim. The room cheered. He turned, faced the crowd, and gave a brief bow.

Chad came up beside her.

Katherine forced her gaze to her brother. "How'd it go?"

He shrugged. "Not bad. Big Napoléon here got everyone straight this morning."

"Big Napoléon?"

Chad grinned, pleased with himself. "Yeah. It's my new nickname for him. Pretty clever, huh?"

"Very clever," Katherine said. "Have you shared it with Al?"

"Hell, no. I'm not an idiot. He's great with a sword, and I've got strong survival instincts. Which," he added darkly, "is why I didn't drink any coffee this morning. Al fixed it, and it tasted like sh—" He broke off, glancing over his shoulder at the wide-eyed children who stood behind them. He lowered his voice. "Horrible. If you have an ounce of concern for my health or our coffeemaker, you'll make it before he does."

Katherine laughed. "Okay. I hear you."

Chad looked at Al again. "We ought to get him to be a pirate in that skit we always used to do." Chad paused. "He's looking at you."

Her chest tightened. "I'll ask him about the skit," she said. She didn't want to look at Al. She was afraid that she would turn into a quivering mass of Jell-O.

"He's still looking at you."

"Thank's for telling me," she muttered, resigning herself. *Time to face the music, chickie.* Anticipation is usually worse than reality, she told herself.

When she looked up and met his deep, dark gaze, though, her heart seemed to stop. Standing tall, with that sword in his hand, he looked every inch the conquering male. But his eyes were tentative, asking, not demanding, and her defenses melted like butter in the sun.

He held out his hand for her to join him.

She didn't hesitate. She'd have to think about that later. She just walked forward and let him take her hand. He held it firmly and whispered in her ear, "How did it go with Logan?"

"Horrible," she said, relieved he wasn't going to refer to what had happened between them last night. "I—I didn't know you could fence."

His jaw tightened, but he kept his voice light. "There are many things you don't know about me."

Katherine trembled and pulled her hand away. She didn't like the way she felt—light-headed, flushed, out of control. And he'd merely touched her hand. "How true," she returned.

He must have felt her response. Al smiled slowly, all male confidence now. "You can trust me."

Katherine shook her head. "I don't know that."

"You need me," he insisted.

"Pirate Island needs you," she corrected. "We'd like you to be a pirate in our Wednesday-night skit. The guests have missed it. Uncle Jasper always co-ordinated it before. We've got a bunch of new employees this year, so no one knows how to pull it off. You could coach the others in fencing, and Chad could direct."

Al flicked the sword through the air thoughtfully. She noticed it was one that had been hanging on the wall. "What do I get in return?" he finally asked.

Her chest felt tight at the look in his eyes. "What do you want?"

"Your trust."

She shook her head automatically. He might as well ask for one of her lungs.

"No." He lifted his shoulders in a masculine shrug. "What a shame. You'll have to find someone else."

Exasperation swept through her. "But—"

"You're not being equitable. You want something from me when you'll give me nothing."

"I'll pay you," Katherine offered.

The children began to get restless. "Do the sword again, Mr. Al," one called.

"Yeah, do it again," another one said.

"It's up to you," Al said to Katherine.

The kids got louder, and Katherine vacillated. This was crazy. She hardly knew the man.

"I can't," she whispered.

"Then I guess we're at a stalemate." He turned to the children. "That's all for today, kids. Talk to Katherine if you want to learn more. She's in charge."

Past a chorus of moans and protests, she glared at him.

He grinned.

Fearing a riot, she grabbed his arm as he began to leave. "There's got to be something else you want." She cringed at how suggestive that sounded. "Something like Saturday nights off, or the use of my car."

He thought it over for a moment and nodded. "Saturday nights off, yes. And the use of your car. Add one more thing."

"What?" she asked suspiciously.

"Answer my questions."

Katherine was nonplussed. She'd been certain he'd ask for something more, perhaps something provocative.

"Katherine?" Al prompted.

Heat scorched her cheeks, and she drew a breath of thanks that he couldn't read minds. Answering questions wasn't difficult. After all, she'd led a pretty boring life except for her brief marriage, and she'd developed a pat uninformative response due to countless inquiries she'd received from reporters. It seemed harmless enough. Two children pulled on her leg and asked for cookies.

Katherine shrugged. "Fine."

He gave her a devastating smile and garnered the attention of the entire room simply by clapping his hands together and picking up the sword. He had such a powerful, commanding presence that even she was awed. The cookies were forgotten, and Katherine wondered again what she'd just gotten herself into.

That evening Katherine skipped her late-night swim and watched a movie on television. Since Chad was in hot pursuit of Suzanne, Katherine and Al shared the evening together.

It should have been comfortable. After a long, hot bath and dinner, she should have been happy and relaxed. They both sat on the plaid sofa, she on one end, he on the other. But Al's proximity unsettled her, and her gaze kept wandering to him.

His hair was damp and ruffled from a shower. He'd changed into a pair of khaki canvas shorts and a yellow pullover. There was nothing seductive about his clothing. Still, she noticed how the yellow of his shirt contrasted with his tanned skin. The gap left by his open collar hinted at the dark chest hair beneath.

Her gaze fell to muscled legs brushed with brown hair. His powerful thighs spread wide in a typically male position. Remembering how he'd felt pressed against her, she felt a rush of heat.

Mentally cursing, Katherine sighed and forced her attention back to the TV.

"Bored?" Al asked.

"No. I guess I'm just tired," she said, keeping her gaze trained on the screen.

"You've earned it. You never told me what Logan had to say." Al turned away from the TV and faced her.

"Now that would bore you." Katherine smiled grimly.

"Are you welshing on our agreement?"

Katherine looked at him. He appeared displeased. "Welshing?"

"You agreed to answer my questions," he pointed out.

"Oh."

"I'm waiting."

Katherine thought about making an early night of it, but her conscience won. She sighed again. "Okay, you want to hear about James Logan. Well, the man nearly drove me crazy."

For the next half hour Katherine gave Al an earful, fully expecting him to yawn, excuse himself, or fall asleep. Instead, he listened carefully, occasionally making suggestions or grinning at something she'd described. The movie forgotten, his attention was focused on her. The way his dark gaze fastened on her made her wish she was beautiful.

"You'll have other options," he assured her at the end of the conversation.

"I hope so. Thanks for listening."

"Even though I had to push you to talk about it."

Her smile broadened. "Yes. But speaking of questions, I'm curious. Where did you learn to fence? England?"

He looked away. "There are other places."

"I've always wanted to visit England," Katherine ventured. "Were you there on business?"

"Yes," he said tersely. "I have another question."

That brought her up short. "Oh." At a temporary loss, she shrugged, expecting something about the campground. "Okay. What is it?"

He looked her over in a way that curled her toes into the sofa cushion. She fought the urge to fold her arms over her chest.

"Where are your lovers?" he finally asked in a rough voice.

Katherine's eyes rounded. "What?" she choked.

"Your lovers," he said impatiently, and stood. "A woman who looks like you, who acts like you, must have lovers. I've watched every man with you, but you don't give off the signals of a woman involved with any of them." He walked the length of the carpet as he tried to solve the quiz.

Speechless, she watched him with dumbfounded astonishment.

"I wondered about Rich."

"Rich!"

Al continued as if she hadn't spoken. "He watches you. He tries to find excuses to touch you. And when you leave, he mutters what a shame it is that you braid your hair. And if only you weren't old Jasper's niece."

"Rich?" Katherine said again weakly. She'd had no idea the dockmaster felt that way.

"You don't watch Rich." Al planted his hands on his hips and stopped directly in front of her.

She shrank against the back of the sofa.

"The only free time you have is when you take your evening swims. Do you meet someone then?"

He asked the question imperiously, as if it were his God-given right to know. Indignation replaced shock. "That's none of your business," she snapped.

He scowled. "You didn't answer my question."

"I'm not going to."

"You agreed," he reminded her.

Katherine felt trapped. She took a deep breath. "So I did." And did she ever regret it. "I do not meet anyone when I swim, because I want to be alone then."

"Then where are your lovers, Katherine?"

Anger swept through her. She scooted off the sofa and around Al. "They're not here!"

She couldn't bring herself to say her lovers were nonexistent. The painful truth was that Katherine had never felt particularly confident of her ability to attract members of the opposite sex, and her disastrous marriage hadn't helped matters.

Her resentment grew. She didn't like her inadequacies thrown in her face. "Why are you asking me these questions? Are you trying to humiliate me? I know I'm not the type to win beauty contests, but do you have to rub it in?" Barely taking a breath, she continued, "Is that what last night was all about? Give Katie a little thrill. She needs it. Well, you can take your drop-dead good looks and your breath-stealing kisses somewhere else. Just leave me the hell alone."

His expression of shock failed to penetrate her fury. She spun around to leave when her shoulder was grabbed roughly from behind.

Al turned her back around and put a finger beneath her chin, forcing her gaze to meet his. His eyes glinted with turbulent emotion. "I don't call you Katie," he told her in a low, velvet voice. "You asked me to call you Katherine."

In spite of her anger, her heart softened a fraction. She'd noticed he called her Katherine. She preferred it. "Yes," she conceded, and let out a breath.

"*Mon Dieu!* I can't begin to understand any of this nonsense about humiliating you." He shook his head as if to clear the irrational thought from his mind, then narrowed his eyes. "As for last night, you felt my heat, and I felt yours. Last night was about me wanting you and you wanting me. If you have any doubts, I can demonstrate it more graphically."

Her heart beat frantically. She felt her face burn. Unable to bear the intensity of his words, she looked away. Still, her hands rested on his bare, muscular arms, and she could feel his strength. Part of her wanted to lean into him, to test his power and feel his passion. But she didn't trust him or herself.

Katherine was out of her depth. "Last night was an accident," she said in a breathless voice.

"No, *mon amie*," he assured her in a soothing male tone that sent awareness skittering through her. "Last night was just the beginning."

She broke away, shaking her head frantically. "No. Absolutely not."

Al stepped forward. "You're scared."

Katherine's defenses rose three feet. "I don't want this."

"You want more than—"

Chad opened the back door and burst into the room. His face was a picture of disgust. "That Suzanne may be easy on the eyes, but she's hell on the ego."

Katherine latched on to his entrance as if it were a lifeline. "I'm going to bed. Lock up." She walked toward her bedroom, calling "good night" over her shoulder.

Chad stared after her, then looked at Alex. "What's her problem?"

Alex shrugged, searching for his next words. "Your sister's a bit skittish."

Nodding in agreement, Chad pulled off his wet jacket and let it drop to the floor.

Alex looked pointedly from the jacket to Chad.

The younger man picked up the jacket and hung it in the closet. "She probably thinks you're a con man," he said, closing the door. "And to Katherine the only thing worse than a con man is a politician. Her father was a con man. Her husband was a politician."

Alex felt as if he'd just been struck. "Husband. She's married?"

"Was. Past tense," Chad said as he ambled to the

lounger and slumped into it. "The guy was a real jerk. She met him at a banquet when she received the Teacher of the Year award."

"So you thought he was a jerk." Al led the conversation where he wanted it to go.

"Yeah. Robert's daddy had big bucks, but he wasn't real happy with Robert's . . . lack of productivity. Robert probably wrecked one too many Ferraris." Chad yawned hugely. "Anyway, his daddy pushed Robert into the political arena. The guy did pretty well. He was getting ready to run for state senate, and he needed an appropriate wife. Katie fit the bill.

"When Robert's daddy kicked the bucket, though, Robert inherited all that money, ditched his political career, and went to Monte Carlo with an exotic dancer. The scandal sheets had a field day." Chad's lower lip curled. "I could have killed him."

Chad sighed and looked at Alex. "Katie'll probably kill me if she finds out I told you this."

"She might," he said absently, feeling not a smidgen of remorse for prying into Katherine's past. He was still absorbing this new information about Katherine. The idea of her being married bothered him. He wondered if she still loved the man. "If he was such a jerk, why did she get involved with him?"

"Katie's got this thing about stability," Chad offered. "I think Robert pulled a real snow job over her." Chad went silent for a moment, then looked uncomfortable. "You aren't trying to put the make on her, are you? She's had enough bums in her life."

Impatient with Chad's assessment of his character, Alex walked to the door and locked it. "That's between your sister and me," he said in dismissal.

A woman who'd been burned required a different approach, he realized. Alex also realized that he wanted something from Katherine, with a wanting so fierce, it bordered on need, though he automatically rejected the idea of needing anyone. Robert's foolish rejection of her suited Alex's purposes. He wasted no pity on the stupidity of Katherine's former husband. Right now, he just wanted to be alone to think.

Chad rose from the chair and stood. "I gotta tell you," he said in the most serious voice Alex had ever heard him use, "that I'll beat you to a pulp if you hurt Katie."

Alex stopped. Surprise warred with irritation. After all, Chad was several inches shorter and about thirty pounds lighter than Alex. His estimation of Chad rose a notch. "If I hurt Katherine, I may just let you," he finally replied.

For the next few days Katherine avoided Al. By taking breakfast in her uncle's office, she made the coffee and managed to get out of the house before Al rose in the mornings. She made a point of not being wherever he was. And if he showed up, she found a reason to leave.

The thought came to her that she was being cowardly, but she brushed it aside. Al had shaken her. When she regained her composure, her control, she'd be able to deal with him more normally. It was just taking longer than she'd expected.

Wednesday night arrived, and Chad and Al were ready to present the pirate skit, although Chad warned her it wouldn't be perfect.

Katherine was delighted. It was a beautiful night. The sea reflected the full moon, and a breeze teased the hem of her sundress. Anticipation simmered among the large group gathered on the beach to watch the drama. Chad had enlisted the help of several guests.

The ship, a replica of an old English shipping vessel, was anchored at the marina with spotlights focused on it. A hush descended over the crowd when the lights dimmed and brightened twice. The scene opened with the English lord Richard, played by Chad, and Lady Bettina, played by Suzanne, dressed in period clothing and engaged in a heated argument.

Katherine grinned at the similarity of art to life. Those two had been at each other's throats lately.

"I don't wish to marry Lord Barrymore," Lady Bettina said loudly.

"Your wishes don't matter, Sister. This is a business arrangement. Lord Barrymore has agreed to keep his promise, even though you have disgraced the entire family by taking off with this pirate Raven." Richard looked down his nose at Bettina. "I fear you're touched in the head since you've become acquainted with Raven."

Bettina tossed her head of long blond curls. "Think what you will. I would sooner die than marry Lord Barrymore."

"The only one sure to die is your Raven. My men have taken him to the local sheriff," Richard returned.

Bettina promptly burst into tears and went below deck.

The audience's sympathy turned against Richard. When he kicked a deckhand's bucket in a fit of temper, the crowd booed. Richard ordered a watch and went to his quarters for the night.

The lights dimmed, and after the sailors settled down, sounds of snoring came over the P.A. system.

The crowd's chuckles were followed by whispers as a group of rowboats silently made its way toward the ship. Led by a tall man in black pants and open, flowing white shirt, a gang of pirates climbed up the side of the boat. Katherine's heart tightened in spite of herself. It was Al with a bandana around his dark head and a sword in his hand.

He gave a loud call to battle, and chaos erupted. Gunshots were fired. The clash of steel, a cry for mercy, and a man's groan were heard. Katherine watched them throw a sailor overboard. The pirates fought viciously, or so it appeared. Along with everyone else, she heard an "Ouch! Watch it!"

The audience, transfixed by the scene, laughed.

Suddenly Lord Richard appeared with sword in hand.

Raven leaped from the side of the ship to stand in front of him. "I've come to collect my treasure, Lord Richard."

Lord Richard shook his head. "We carry no gold, Raven. Take your leave. You've caused enough mischief tonight."

Raven laughed, tossing back his head, revealing strong white teeth. "'Tis not gold I seek, you fool. 'Tis Bettina."

Katherine's breath caught at the sight of him. His strength and power were revealed with none of the trappings of civilization and all the glory of his basic masculinity. She could almost feel the heat of him.

Lord Richard raised his sword. Light reflected off the flashing steel. The men parried and thrust, lunged and feinted.

Roused by the noise, Bettina entered.

At her cry Raven turned to see her, taking a cutting stroke to his arm. When dark blood seeped into his shirt, the crowd gasped. Katherine did, too, even though she knew it couldn't be real.

Raven turned the full strength of his fury against Richard. In the blink of an eye Richard was disarmed, and the point of Raven's sword rested against Richard's throat.

Bettina ran to Raven. "Have mercy on him. He is a fool, but he is my brother."

Raven paused, keeping his sword poised on the utterly still Richard.

Everyone held his breath.

"Away with him!" Raven ordered his men, and watched them take Richard below.

Raven took Bettina in his arms and kissed her soundly.

The audience whistled and cheered. But the enjoyment ended right there for Katherine. Her mouth went dry as dust. She watched Al's firm mouth pressed against Suzanne's and felt a painful wrenching inside. A shiver ran down her spine.

The campers gave an enthusiastic ovation and congratulated Katherine on the success of the skit. Some returned to their campsites. Others gathered around for the scheduled "Dancing on the Beach."

It was just a corny little drama for the guests, she told herself later. She should be pleased by its success. Chad and Al had been surrounded by admirers for the past hour. The notion that she was jealous appalled her. She wasn't that kind of person. Katherine sighed and looked at the ocean.

"Will you dance with me, Katie?"

She turned. It was Tom, the mechanic. He was a shy, thin man with brown hair and kind hazel eyes. She knew for a fact that he was five years older than she was, but he seemed younger. Katherine mustered a smile. "Of course. Thank you," she said, and allowed him to lead her into the gyrating fray.

The next song was a slow one, and she was about to excuse herself when Al appeared. Still dressed in his pirate's costume, he was dangerously compelling.

"Dance with me," he said in that arrogant tone that still made her blink.

She took a deep breath. "Well, I was just about to—"

"—dance with me," he finished with a maddening smile.

Katherine stepped backward at the intensity in his dark eyes. "I don't think— Oops." She bumped into another couple. "Excuse me."

Al pulled her into his arms. "I've been looking for you."

Her heart jumped. "I've been here all night long." *Time to move away, Katherine.*

"But not close enough." His fingers sifted through her hair, and for an instant she imagined his hands all over her.

She swallowed. "Al, I don't think this is a good idea," Katherine began.

He brushed her hair behind her bare shoulder,

his gaze falling to her skin. The way he looked at her, she could almost believe he found her beautiful. The notion was so tantalizing that her impulse to flee died instantly. She shivered.

"It's an excellent idea. You told me I need to learn how to have fun." He drew her closer and lowered his mouth to her ear. Their swaying movements brought his thighs against hers, rubbing, stroking. Hard against soft. He parted her legs with one of his, his thigh connecting with her in melting intimacy.

His voice was deep and rich with promise. "I want you to teach me."

FOUR

Katherine looked at Al and swallowed a lump in her throat that felt like a watermelon. Yeah, right, she thought. The gap between her "experience" and his would rival the Grand Canyon.

She wanted to wipe that "I'm gonna eat you alive" smile off his face, but his attention was fixed on her in a way that both frightened and fascinated her. And that damn music was playing in her mind again. She shook her head to clear it, to swat the melody that hummed like a persistent fly.

The music was sweet and poignant, full of rich memories and hope. Al guided her into a turn, and suddenly it hit her.

"Paganini!" she whispered.

He frowned. "What?"

"Paganini! The broken music box." She stared at him in comprehension. "You're the man on the music box."

Thoroughly confused, Al stopped. "Paganini?"

"No. You're the man on my music box." She laughed in relief. "I'm not going crazy. I kept hearing this music whenever you were close, but I couldn't put my finger on the tune. It's Paganini."

Alex was sure there was something he was missing. He looked at her blankly. She stepped away. Immediately feeling the loss, he reached for her hand. "I've been called many things, but never Paganini and never the man on a music box." He gestured away from the crowd. "Let's walk on the beach, and you can explain."

Katherine hesitated, then smiled sheepishly. "I guess I owe you that much. Let me get rid of these shoes." She kicked them off and carried them with her free hand.

They walked silently for a few moments. Her hand was small within his. The physical connection wasn't much, but it affected him. It made him think of things he'd wanted and never had. Al had walked on a moonlit beach before, but tonight seemed new, filled with stars, the murmur of waves, and a magic he would have sworn didn't exist.

"When I was ten years old," she began, "my mother got married for the third time. She spent the summer in the Caribbean, and I was left feeling neglected and sorry for myself."

He laced his fingers through hers more tightly,

remembering the same feeling during his childhood. "Sounds understandable."

"Yes, well, I was very disillusioned about this romance stuff. Too cynical for such a young girl. I think Uncle Jasper wanted to preserve the idea of forever, happily-ever-after love in my impressionable mind a little longer." She looked into the distance and smiled. "He bought me this antique music box, and it played a tune by Paganini."

"And?"

"And there was a procelain man and woman dancing on the top of it. Round and round they went. I used to wind it and watch them for hours. The woman was beautiful, with perfect features." Her lips twitched. "Gleaming blond hair. I would have dyed my hair that summer if I'd known how."

"I'm glad you didn't," said Al, appalled. "Your hair is beautiful as it is."

Disbelief flickered in her eyes, warring with trust. It frustrated Al, but he wanted to hear the rest of the tale. "And the man?"

She looked away. "He was very handsome. I remember imagining that he would be strong, yet gentle. He had dark hair and dark eyes. Those eyes of his never left the face of the woman. His gaze didn't wander. He didn't grow bored. He adored her." She seemed to realize what she'd revealed about herself and made a show of shrugging it off.

"I pretended I was the woman. I was just ten, and

you know how children can be. Full of daydreams."

Al didn't know how children could be. His formative years had been spent in such constraint, partly because of his position, partly because of his father's mistakes.

"My family has had their share of problems," he admitted. "My father made a mistake that hurt my mother. It ended up hurting all of us. My sisters and I could have had a much different childhood. Instead . . ."

Katherine heard the unspoken longing and loss. It struck a chord in her. "So, you have sisters?"

"Yes. We were separated for almost seven years. I—" He hesitated, because he'd never openly discussed the subject. Katherine didn't know of his position, though, and it seemed a good opportunity to for once share the burden of his childhood. "—I missed them."

She stopped, dropping her sandals to the sand, then tentatively lifted a hand to his arm. "I'm sure you did. Seven years. That's half a childhood."

His throat felt thick with emotion. It was a disconcerting sensation. He swallowed hard and nodded, hoping it would pass.

"Sometimes it's hard for me to imagine you as a child. You're so serious." She searched his face with open, guileless eyes. Her hand fluttered like a butterfly against his skin. "After hearing this, I think I understand. Don't worry. I won't ask you to tell me more than you already have, but . . ." She paused, giving a heavy sigh. "It's feeble and small, and it won't change a thing, but I'm sorry, really sorry."

Her comfort and concern washed over him, through a crack into a deep, dark part of him. Pity he could have fought, but not this gentle honesty. It struck him again what a generous, open woman Katherine was. It hit him hard again, the overwhelming urge to possess her and know her, in every way.

"You're a remarkable woman," he murmured.

Katherine's heart jerked in her chest. Again, she sensed a deep loneliness inside him, and it hurt her to see it. The moment grew heavy, fraught with tension. It was too intimate, but she'd done it again, stuck her heart in where it didn't belong. She shied away. "Not really. Look at how loony I've been acting around you. I'm just relieved to know why. Bet you are too," she finished dryly.

"You think this connection between us is because of the music box?"

She looked down at the sand and dug her toes into it. "Well, of course. I mean, it's a logical explanation, don't you think?" She didn't wait for him to answer. "Yes. It makes perfect sense."

"Then you needn't fear me."

She opened her mouth to argue, then closed it.

He raised their twined hands and brushed the back of her hand with his lips. He smiled.

Her heart dipped.

"So, you will teach me to play."

She gave a shaky laugh. "I'm not sure I'm the right woman to teach you what you want to learn."

"You're the only woman to teach me what I want to learn."

She shook her head. "I don't think—"

He gave her a gentle but impatient shake. "Then don't think. Trust me. Teach me. I'm an exceptional student. My marks were superior. I was my professors' best and brightest." He'd damn well had to be.

Katherine laughed in spite of herself. "Okay! Okay! Have you ever heard of the word 'humility'?"

"I think I read it once or twice," he deadpanned.

She rolled her eyes. "Okay, Al Sanders. I'm the toughest first-grade teacher at Greenfield Elementary. I hope you know what you're getting into."

He didn't have a clue, but as he watched the light in her eyes and the wind through her hair, he sure as hell wanted to find out.

"Nobody else will do it," Chad said. "So you've got to."

Katherine wavered, then thought about the greased flagpole and shook her head. "This was *your* lunatic idea. Find someone else. There must be a teenager in that crowd whose fondest wish is to climb on top of a bunch of men and get a tin can off the top of a greased flagpole."

"I've already tried. Besides, you asked me to come up with something new and physically challenging. The least you can do is show some support."

Chad was marginally right, she knew. Katherine exhaled with such force, it ruffled her bangs. "There's got to be somebody," she muttered.

Chad must have sensed her weakening. "You. You're light and agile. You've got great balance. The—"

"The two teams are ready," Al said from the open doorway. "Have you found someone to climb to the top yet?"

Chad threw Katherine a meaningful glance. "Yes, but she's reluctant."

Just seeing Al brought a flutter to her stomach. She deliberately looked away from him. "Okay, Chad. I'll do it. But you owe me for this one."

Al looked from Chad to Katherine, and an expression of disbelief crossed his face. "Not Katherine."

Chad shrugged. "She's perfect for the job. She used to take gymnastics. She's light and agile. Plus, the guests will love it."

Al dismissed it. "She might get hurt. We'll get someone else. She can be the referee."

"We'll have some people to spot," Chad argued.

"And what if they miss?"

"Just a minute." Katherine frowned. They were talking about her as if she weren't there. "I've already told Chad I'd do it. You're not *telling* me I can't, are you?"

"You might get hurt," Al explained. "You're not strong enough."

Chad snickered.

Katherine and Al glared at him.

He cleared his throat, stifling his amusement. "I, uh, think I'll go outside with the guests."

A twinge of irritation compounded by lack of sleep twisted through her.

Al's gaze probed hers. "You don't really want to do this."

She shifted. "That's not the point."

"You're right," he said with a nod. "The point is that you have no business crawling on top of nine men to reach the top of a flagpole."

Katherine grinned in amusement. "Oh, I don't know. Some women might find the image of having nine men at their feet appealing."

Al's mouth firmed into a straight line. "I won't allow you to do this." He turned to leave as if his was the final word.

Katherine's eyes opened wide. For a moment she was speechless. Where did he get the nerve to order her as if she were one of his employees instead of the other way around? Where did he get the right? Her temperature rose. This wasn't the first time he'd pulled this. She tore after him. "I'm doing it. You've got this all confused, Al. I don't take orders from you. I give them to you."

He stopped and half turned.

"You can't order me not to climb that flagpole. Do you hear me? You can't order me around."

His displeasure was almost a tangible thing. He looked big and very ticked off. At this moment no one in his right mind would cross him.

Katherine, however, wasn't in her right mind. His imperious attitude galled her, and it didn't help that she kept catching herself humming Paganini every time she turned around. She poked her freshly manicured finger into his concrete chest. "Just because you're a big man and I'm a small woman doesn't mean you can push me around."

He raised an eyebrow and glanced down at her impertinent finger. Abruptly aware of the chest beneath her finger, she cleared her throat and told herself to take a quick megastep back, but her feet wouldn't cooperate.

"I have no desire to push you around, *mon amie*," he said in a low, sexy voice. "Not until we're in bed. In that case I'll be very glad you're female, and I'll expect you to push back. It will be"—he paused and the devil came into his eyes—"more *fun* that way, no?"

Katherine sucked in a quick breath and stumbled

backward. She couldn't think about being in bed with him. The idea would leave her boneless for a week. "You're twisting everything I say. The campers are waiting, and I'm going to climb that flagpole."

"You will not."

"I will, and you'll have nothing to do with it." She marched around him and felt him stalking her all the way to the harbor.

Katherine wasn't sure exactly how it happened, but within minutes it was all arranged. She would climb the flagpole, but Al would be the one holding her on top of two layers of men when she grabbed the tin can.

Suzanne blew the whistle, and the two teams scrambled into action. Six stout, medium-height men locked arms around the bottom of the flagpole. Immediately Chad, Al, and one other man began climbing on top of them to form the second tier.

She glanced over at the other team, which was mostly teenage boys, and laughed at the comments filtering through the groans and grunts.

"Get your foot out of my face! I can't breathe."

"Quit wiggling. I might as well have Jell-O under my feet."

"Jell-O would sure as hell smell better than your feet."

Then she heard a stocky fellow from her own

team yell, "Chad, your heel is in my Adam's apple. I swear I'm gonna rip it off if you—"

"Okay, okay." Chad shifted. "Katie, get the lead out. We're ready."

For just a second, when she looked at the way the men swayed and moved, a sliver of apprehension crept in, and she thought about what Al had said about her safety. Then she noticed the high-flyer for the other team starting to climb, and her competitive spirit took over.

She ran to the shortest man and smiled apologetically. "I'll try not to hurt you."

He nodded.

She climbed up his back and wobbled onto his shoulders. "Chad, you're next."

"Go ahead."

"I'm going to put my foot on your waist and try to swing up."

Chad ground his teeth. "Just shut up and do it."

Katherine got the first part right, but he started to sway. Her heart clenched. "Chad! You can't move."

"I have to move a little. You know, Katie, you weigh more than I thought you did."

He swayed again, and her hands started to sweat. Seeing Al's rock-solid form beside her, she reconsidered her options. "I'm going to try Al."

"Then hurry up. I think the other team is gaining, and I don't want to lug all those people into the harbor."

"Harbor?" she said faintly as she slid back down. Her foot connected with somebody's head. "Oops. Sorry."

"Lock your arms around my neck and wrap your legs around my waist," Al said in a clear, calm voice.

Katherine shifted and stretched, reaching for his shoulders.

"What's wrong?"

Frustration warred with fear. She wanted this to be over. "You're too tall."

He groaned but bent slightly to accommodate her, and she hitched herself up. She pressed her face into his neck for just a moment, relishing the security.

Al felt her breath against his skin. Her breasts plastered to his back, and her thighs molded to his hard hips. It was as close as she'd ever been to him, and it was all wrong. They shouldn't be up here. They should be in bed. On a table. On the floor. Hell, he wasn't picky. He'd even risk the discomfort of sand for her.

He sensed her fear. "You don't have to finish this if you don't want to."

"Yes, I do," she said through gritted teeth, slowly moving her feet to either side of his hips. "It's just that the ground is farther away than I planned."

Al licked his lips to keep from grinning. He bit his tongue. He would not say "I told you so."

"And don't you dare say I told you so!"

A chuckle escaped. "It's difficult to say anything with the death grip you have on my throat."

"Hey, are y'all having a tea party up there, or what?" called one of the foundation men.

More grumbles and groans followed.

"Okay, okay," Katherine whispered. She was wet with perspiration. The afternoon sun beat down so mercilessly, she was sure she had freckles forming on the inside of her eyelids. She lost her footing and let out a panicky whimper. Al's hand latched over her wrist.

"Whatever you do," he said, "lean forward. I won't let you fall."

Somewhere inside her she must have believed him, because her heart stopped pounding, and she felt calmed, almost safe. She scrambled up until she was sitting on his shoulders, then standing. Whoever had coated the pole with Crisco had done his job well. She hugged the warm, slippery metal and saw the ferry in the far distance. She had an odd sensation, looking down at the tops of trees.

Her foundation shifted, and Katherine was jerked back to reality. She stretched her fingers up to the can and slipped it off. "I got it!"

The onlookers whistled and cheered. The other team booed.

Katherine sat down hard on Al's shoulders.

"Take your time," he said, holding her thigh.

For a half-second she thought about how right his hands felt on her.

Then she shook her head. High altitude, she told herself. She scooted down, hopped off, and the pyramid collapsed.

Her feet barely touched the ground before Rich hauled her up in his arms.

"What in—"

He smiled. "Rules of the game. Winners get dunked in the harbor."

Katherine glared at him, struggling against his hold. "Then why did I try so hard?" she muttered.

Rich just laughed and tightened his grip. "So you wouldn't have to carry all the other team's men to the water!"

Then Katherine was sailing through the air and into the water. When she surfaced, she heard more splashes, hoots, and hollers, and a loud argument between Rich and Al. Blinking the cool water from her eyes, she spotted them. Al had Rich by the collar and looked ready to jerk a knot in the dockmaster.

"It's just part of the game!" Rich said.

Katherine groaned and kicked her way closer to shore. "Al, they're throwing all the winners in," she yelled. She pointed at Chad getting his due. "Look at Chad."

Al paused but didn't let go of Rich. He looked at Chad first, then at Katherine in complete confusion. "It's part of the game?"

She gave a big nod and smiled. "Now, it's your turn."

He abruptly noticed the three men standing expectantly by his side. "Me?"

They nodded.

Al gave Rich a hard glare, released his shirt, then sighed and nodded to the waiting culprits. They picked Al up and threw him in the water.

Trying to conceal her laughter, Katherine swam to Al's side when he surfaced.

"You think this is funny," he growled.

The giggle bubbled out. "Very." She laughed again helplessly. "You look so stern."

He fought a grin. "Then why are you laughing?"

"You look so stern." Another giggle. She took in a mouthful of water that time. "And so wet."

"Come here," he said around his own chuckle.

He dragged her close, so that her slick body rubbed against his. Her breath caught. "Stop," she protested. "I feel like a greased pig."

He shook his head, his hair blacker than ever. She was close enough to see the way the water made his eyelashes spiky. "Not a pig."

He wrapped one hand on her back, and Katherine's hands automatically went to his chest. The water lost its cooling effect.

His thin wet cotton shirt revealed more than concealed the contours beneath, the hard muscles, swirls of dark hair, and male nipples puckered against the cold. She felt the strongest urge to rip the shirt off and bury her face there, to inhale his scent, feel his skin against her cheek, to taste him. A quiver rippled through her.

She tore her gaze from his chest. "Well," she said brightly, trying to recapture a lighter mood. "Did you have fun?"

He looked at her oddly, as if he were puzzling over her behavior. "You mean, did I enjoy getting thrown in the water?"

The thud of his heartbeat beneath her palm distracted her. She cleared her throat. "Well, that and the flagpole race. All of it."

"All of it," he mused, bringing her tighter against him. His eyelids lowered sensuously. "I don't know about all of it, Katherine. But I believe getting thrown in the water with you definitely has its compensations." He glanced at her breasts.

Katherine's gaze shot down to what had become a peekaboo shirt and felt her cheeks burn. "Oh, no," she moaned.

He had the nerve to laugh.

She glared.

"Oh, yes," he said, and dunked her before she could hit him.

The next morning Katherine was up at the ungodly hour of four-thirty. All part of Al's recreational education, she thought with a grimace as they baited their hooks.

"It's quiet," Al said, and cast his line.

"Yes. I'd counted on Chad to come with us." As a chaperon, her conscience baited her. She frowned. "He's usually more talkative in the morning than I am."

"Except when he stays at Chuck's too long and wakes up with a hangover."

"Right," she said dryly, and cast her line.

"What made you decide on fishing?"

She yawned. "Well, I've been analyzing your fun . . ." She thought for a moment and smiled. "Your fun disability."

He turned his head at that. "Disability!"

Katherine nodded. "Yes, that's exactly what it is. It appears that you always need to have some sort of active goal in order to have fun. And what I've decided is that you need to learn to enjoy the *process* of having fun."

Leaning closer to her, he whispered. "Isn't the goal of fishing to catch a fish?"

His whisper sent a hot shiver through her. She leaned away and propped her fishing pole in the bracket. "Some people would say that. But I think the goal of fishing is to enjoy the quiet." She slapped at a mosquito. "In spite of the bugs."

"All right," he said, and wondered what was in her head this morning. She'd seemed inordinately upset when Chad couldn't go with them. Al put his fishing pole in a bracket, then eased onto his back.

He watched her hug her knees to her chest, her hair flowing freely over her back. She looked into the dark horizon, humming softly under her breath. He felt a strange protectiveness surge through him.

Fingers burning to touch her long curls, he gave in to the inclination and fondled a strand. The humming stopped. He was oddly disappointed. "What were you singing?"

She paused, then moaned. "Oh, not again." She sighed and flipped her hand through her hair. "Nothing, really. Just a little tune I learned a long time ago."

She seemed uncomfortable. It frustrated him. He wanted her free and easy with him. He gave her hair a gentle tug. "Is it the Paganini?"

Slowly she turned. Her wary gaze caught his. "Yes," she admitted.

He tangled more of her hair in his fingers. "I'd like to see this music box. Will you show me?"

"It's broken."

"But you still have it."

She nodded, and he sensed her wariness. The music box represented her most cherished dreams. "Is it in the cottage?"

Hesitantly she nodded again. "In my closet." She hadn't looked at it in years, but she knew it was still there in a box. She shrugged. "I doubt you'd be impressed with an old broken music box."

He moved closer. His hand was still on her hair, and his scent seemed to fill her senses. The morning was cool, and she found herself wanting to lean into his masculine warmth. He reached for her hand, turned it over, and drew slow circles on her palm. Her breasts immediately tightened. She was glad it was still dark, and he couldn't see how easily he affected her.

"But will you show me?"

Oh, hell, she thought. It's just a music box. "Okay, okay. Can I have my hand back now?"

"No," he said simply, and brought her fingers to his lips.

She should have jerked her hand away. But mesmerized by the look in his eyes, she didn't move an inch.

His gaze fastened on her, he gave a quick hard tug that pulled her off balance and onto his chest. "You were too far away."

Her heart flipped. "I didn't think so."

"Maybe I can change your mind."

With no further warning he pressed his mouth against hers. His tongue teased and coaxed, and she couldn't help thinking his kisses were richer than Godiva chocolate and just as forbidden. One just wasn't enough. His passion was a dark, potent liquor that punched through her veins, leaving her intoxicated.

He slanted his mouth and shifted so that she lay sprawled on his chest, her legs between his raised knees. His arousal nudged the apex of her thighs, hard and ready. Through their clothing he crushed her breasts to his chest, and his hands urged her bottom in a rocking motion against him. Her heart clenched tight, and she went light-headed. It was just enough to make her wonder if she was going to faint. She made a sound somewhere between a whimper and a moan.

He pulled her away. For a moment she resisted.

He swore, then gave her a quick, hard kiss. "We've got to breathe. Help me out, Katherine."

She slumped to his shoulder and took several minutes to catch her breath. There was no use pretending anymore. "Lord, you can kiss."

"I want to make love to you."

Her breath caught. She was still off balance. "Do we have to? Kissing you's much better than sex."

He looked at her as if she'd lost it. "Don't you like sex?"

She squirmed. "Well, it's not exactly that."

"Katherine." He tilted her chin up so she would meet his gaze. "I think you need to explain."

Her heart sank. She really didn't want to discuss it. She'd revealed far too much already. And this was just too private. He'd never understand, not in a million years.

FIVE

"I'm not good at it," Katherine said.

Alex blinked. Unless he'd missed a switch in the conversation, "it" was sex. "But how—"

She stiffened and tried to ease away, but he held fast. "Don't feel sorry for me. We all have our talents. I'm an excellent first-grade teacher. I'm a decent dancer." She shrugged. "I'm good at a lot of things. I'm just not good at"—she took a deep breath and finished—"sex."

Though she tried to affect a matter-of-fact tone, Alex could hear the misery in her voice. This was a moment that called for all his tact, diplomacy, and understanding. Fury lashed through him, and his voice rose in spite of himself. "What jerk tried to sell you that piece of idiocy?"

Katherine winced and sat up. "Stop yelling! You'll scare away the fish. Nobody had to tell me. I figured it out on my own." She glared at him. "I don't like discussing it. And if you had an ounce of sensitivity, you'd drop the subject."

Alex sat up and positioned his face about a millimeter from hers. "You brought up the subject."

"I did not," she whispered, her eyes turbulent with emotion. "You did when you said you wanted to make love to me."

"That hasn't changed."

She looked down for a long moment, pursing her lips. "Okay, I'll give you the abbreviated version. I was inexperienced when I got married. He'd been involved with some beautiful, worldly women, and I didn't want to disappoint him."

The rising dawn revealed the tension on her face. Alex wanted to wipe it away, but he sensed she was struggling to retain her composure.

"The honeymoon went okay. Nothing earth-shattering, but I figured if I tried, it could get better." She looked out onto the water. "It didn't. When I think back—" She broke off and gave a heavy sigh.

Alex narrowed his eyes. He'd like five minutes alone with her ex-husband. This was the kind of chore he delegated to his security force, but this time he'd trade a slew of his titles for the opportunity to get the man who'd done this to her. "How do you know your husband wasn't at fault?"

She met his gaze and shrugged. "Because he was the experienced one."

"Experienced in what way?" he asked, a hard edge creeping into his voice.

"In the usual way."

"Katherine, every woman is different. What works with one doesn't necessarily work with another. It's the same way for men. A man must discover the hidden desires in his lover."

"I tried to do that," she said earnestly. "I read the *Kama-sutra*. I read *How to Drive Your Man Wild in Bed*. I tried every trick in the book, and it just didn't work."

Al's patience ran out. "Then you married an idiot. Any man who wouldn't be delighted with you 'trying every trick' on him would have to be insane."

"We're not getting anywhere with this discussion."

"If you would trust me instead of—"

Katherine held up her hand. "Oh, no. You're not pulling that autocratic stuff on me again. I know what I went through, and you don't."

The idea of Katherine being with another man made him feel murderous, yet he couldn't leave the issue unsettled. The taste of his questions was bitter on his tongue, but he had to ask them. "Did he hurt you physically?"

"No."

The next question was the toughest. He gritted

his teeth, then deliberately relaxed his jaw. "Did you enjoy making love with him?"

"No! How was I supposed to enjoy something that felt so empty and humiliating? I always felt like he was trying to do me a favor."

He *would* kill the man. "You were married to the wrong man."

"How do you know that?"

He stifled the impulse to tell her to trust him and tried another tactic. "I could always offer for you to try your tricks on me."

"How generous of you," she retorted. "I think I'll pass."

"It's a fair trade. You're teaching me to have fun. I could teach you . . ."

She rolled her eyes. "Teach me the wonders of sex."

Disliking her flip tone, he caught her chin. "No. You know about sex. What you need is to learn how to enjoy making love." He raised an eyebrow. "The *process* of making love."

He caught her attention with that. Katherine could appreciate the idea of enjoying the process. After all, those had been her exact words to Al.

She looked at his face and tried to see into his mind. The hard sculpted lines told the truth of his will and personality. His hair, longer than when he'd first arrived on Pirate Island, invited a women to look past his dark countenance, to weave her fingers, to hold on. His unflinching gaze could burn steel with its intensity. And Lord knows, she wasn't made of steel.

He was too arrogant and too proud. She could have hated him for that arrogance and kept her distance, but he'd shown her the secret of his vulnerability. He was so male, so sexy, and he said he wanted her. It made her heart stop to think of it.

It wouldn't take much for her to give in. But for some reason she couldn't explain even to herself, the stakes were higher this time. Part of it was that she'd lost a piece of herself in her marriage. Part of it was something else, something deeper.

Katherine gave a quick shake of her head, pulling away. She tried for a lighter note. "Your offer's very generous, but I think I'll have to pass."

His gaze narrowed. He didn't like being refused. She'd wager he didn't deal with refusals too often.

His intensity made her nervous. She made a show of reaching for her fishing pole and fussing with it.

"It's going to happen between us."

She shivered at his tone. "It doesn't have to."

"It *will* happen, Katherine. And when it does, you'll beg me to love you again."

She shook her head. "No. I'll be embarrassed and humiliated."

"You'll burn when I come inside you."

Katherine suppressed a shudder and swallowed the lump in her throat.

"I'll find your soft, secret places with my hands, my mouth, with all of me."

Lord help me. Katherine covered her eyes with one hand. He couldn't see the rage going on inside her, the way her breasts drew taut at his words, the way she ached between her thighs. For some men this would be bragging. But with Al she sensed it was an oath. She suspected he was capable of all he promised. But was she?

She pushed back her bangs. "You know, Al, I'm only saving you frustration and disappointment."

His lips played with a grin, but his eyes remained serious. "Then say yes."

She scowled. He'd deliberately misinterpreted her. "No. Besides, we'll both be too busy for"—she waved her hand—"that kind of stuff. You've got the drama tomorrow night, and I just found out the press is coming."

His voice dropped an octave. "The press?"

She was puzzled by his grim expression. "Yes, I thought it might draw in some new prospects."

He looked away, saying nothing. The distance between them had suddenly grown exponentially. A moment later he caught a fish, and she exclaimed over it. "It's huge, and I didn't even catch a minnow. I'll have to hang my head in shame."

Silence followed as he deftly unhooked it. Then he looked at her. "It's time to go back."

Her stomach clenched. She nodded. The warmth in his eyes had turned cool, his manner remote. The easy moments were passed. To her dismay her sense of loss was staggering.

By the following evening she was ready to wring his neck. Swollen with humidity and expectation, the starless cloudy night reflected her edgy mood. "He's around here somewhere," she muttered, looking at the crowd filling the beach in anticipation of the pirate drama. "I don't know where, but I know he's still here."

Chad came up behind her. "How do you know he didn't take a ferry?"

Because the back of my neck tingles as if he's watching me. Because I still hear that blasted music. Because I don't want him gone. Katherine shook her head. "I don't know. I just think he is."

Chad looked at her skeptically. "We're supposed to start in ten minutes, Katie. We've got two reporters, a crowd, and no Raven."

"I know that, Chad," she said, irritation seeping through. "Have you got any brilliant suggestions?"

Chad jammed his hands in his pockets. "No. It's like he disappeared after you two went fishing yesterday." He gave her a curious glance. "What'd you do to the poor guy, anyway?"

Poor guy! Chad's question hit a nerve. Katherine had worried that she'd offended Al yesterday. On top of that, dealing with the reporters all day had made her nervous and edgy. "I didn't do anything to him. How am I supposed to know what's wrong? He's not exactly forthcoming."

"I thought maybe he was more open with you."

"Well, he's not," she said, reminded afresh of how much she didn't know about Al and how much more he knew about her. "Maybe he's not as reliable as we thought."

Chad checked his watch. "Five minutes. I gotta go backstage. I'll try to come up with something."

Katherine forced a smile. "Break a leg."

"Gonna break his neck," he muttered as he hurried away.

Fifteen minutes later the drama was underway, and Katherine wasn't sure if Al had shown up yet. She sent up a hundred prayers.

She inhaled the metallic scent of impending rain. The wind lifting her skirts and her hair echoed a wordless warning. Every muscle in her body was tense. Every nerve was rattled, and her stomach churned. She told herself it was because of the reporters, but part of her knew she wasn't ready for Al to leave. The knowledge unsettled her more.

There was a long pause when Raven was due to make his entrance.

Katherine held her breath.

Then the spotlight caught Raven with his tight black pants, billowy white shirt, gleaming sword, and something new—a black mask. Relief gushed through Katherine. She let out the breath she'd been holding, and the drama continued with near-perfect timing.

This time Katherine looked away when it came time for Al to kiss Suzanne. She knew she was being ridiculous, but she didn't want to see that again.

Afterward, the performers took their bow. Al seemed to be searching the crowd for someone.

Was it for her? Her heart quickened to an embarrassingly fast rate. Digging her toes into the sand, she brushed the thought aside. He was probably looking for those reporters. So much for her ardent lover.

Fat drops of the promised rain began to fall. The crowd broke apart, with everyone headed for their tents or the nearest shelter.

Dawdling under a floodlight, Katherine couldn't resist a last glance at him. For one long moment she'd swear he was looking at her. *What do you want from me?* she wondered. Tension and restraint vibrated from him. Something inside was tearing at him, making him miserable. Couldn't everyone else see it? Why did she? Why did she care? Why did she want to be the one to soothe him?

Whatever he wanted, she couldn't give it. The price was too high.

He came to her in the night and woke her with a gentle kiss. Soon he joined her on her bed with the moonlight streaming through the window. Her clothes dissolved beneath his hands, and he caressed her until she was breathless.

Giving in to her wordless need, he entered her, stretching and filling her. Tears came to her eyes. They were one at last, she thought. Now, she knew him intimately. Then Katherine saw that he was wearing a mask on his face. He was a stranger after all. She lifted her hands and tugged, but the mask wouldn't come off. . . .

Katherine sat straight up in bed. Gasping and disoriented, she looked on either side of her rumpled bed for Al. He wasn't there.

She fumbled, then clicked on her bedside light. Her window was cracked, just as she'd left it. Her door was closed. For a moment she just sat there, breathing hard, trapped in that window between reality and fantasy. It had been so real. She'd heard his voice, felt his lips.

He had been there. In her arms, against her breasts. *Inside her.* Between her legs she felt swollen and stretched, as if . . .

"Oh, no," she moaned. It couldn't be.

Another dream. She must be going crazy. She rubbed her arms, her heart hammering against her chest. Her white cotton gown clung to her damp skin, and her hair stuck to the back of her neck. She lifted it away and shivered.

His scent clung to the air, and the music still played in her head. Her breasts tingled with arousal. Her lips burned.

Desperation bubbled to the surface, and a sob escaped. With shaking hands she covered her mouth. She had to get out of here. It didn't matter that her clock read 2:00 A.M. or that the rain still fell outside her window. She felt trapped, and she had to get out.

Jerking off her gown and pulling on her dress from the night before, Katherine left her bedroom and ran to the beach.

Alex hadn't gone to sleep, hadn't even tried. Distracted, he still wore Raven's shirt and pants. He walked the width of his small bedroom, debating whether he should go ahead and return to Moreno. He'd counted on eluding the press, and it had been a shock to learn they were on Pirate Island by invitation. So, there was the press, his responsibilities to his country, his false identity.

And there was Katherine.

He stiffened, bracing himself against untried emotions rushing through him, threatening to erupt. She made him feel powerful, yet human. How, he wondered, frowning, did she manage it? How could anyone so small affect him so much? Why had such an unworldly woman turned his head? He could never marry her. She was totally unsuitable. Yet he had to possess her. It was becoming an obsession.

The silk mask dangled from the bedpost, mocking him. He swore at it, then crushed it in his hand and threw it out of sight. He was so frustrated, he could have roared.

A click from the front door interrupted his brooding thoughts, and he brushed aside the curtains. He immediately identified the small figure running through the rain. He stood stock-still while his mind raced. He should leave her alone. He should accept her rejection. He should turn his back, blank her out of his mind. He shouldn't follow her.

Alex had spent his life doing what he should, denying himself. What he wanted for Katherine, though, was more powerful than all his shoulds. Discontent rippled through him, taunting and challenging. He pushed away from the window and followed his needs.

Heedless of the rain, he tracked her to the beach. It was only a few strides before he caught her from behind. She was damp and soft and light. Then she turned into a whirling dervish.

She cried out, fighting. "Stop it! Let me go. Let me go."

She rammed an elbow into his side, and he swore, tightening his grip. "Hush! It's me, Alex."

His voice didn't calm her. "Let me go, you, you, you—" Her heel connected with his shin.

The little pain fueled his irritation. Patience gone, he flipped her into his arms so that her face was two inches from his, but her arms and legs were safely bound.

She glared at him. "You *creep*!"

Al frowned. Something was wrong with this picture. He'd imagined her soft and malleable in his arms, not hissing like a she-cat. He opened his mouth, ready to make her take back the insult, but Katherine was just getting started.

"You low-down creep! I was just fine until you came. Get your slimy hands off me."

Creep was one thing, but slimy? He dumped her on the sand. He heard her muttered curses about his father, his grandfather, and his great-grandfather. Al stopped listening after that. "Would you care to explain this irrational display of behavior?"

She scrambled to her feet. "Irrational!" She thumped herself on the chest. "I'm not irrational. I didn't disappear for over twenty-four hours and show up for a performance in a mask, did I?"

Temporarily distracted by the outline of her breasts against her damp dress, he did not respond.

"I didn't assault you from behind when you were minding your own business taking a walk on the beach."

He looked straight into her furious eyes. "I didn't assault you. It's a strange time to stroll on the beach since it's the middle of the night and it's raining."

"Then go back to bed."

"I wasn't in bed. I couldn't sleep for thinking of you."

She sucked in a deep breath. Their gazes locked for a full minute. A full minute with the soft drizzle coming down when need and desire fought against fear. A full minute when he didn't feel lonely because he saw she felt the same way that he did.

Katherine bit her lip and turned away.

His chest went tight. "Wait," he said. When she still wouldn't face him, he swallowed his pride. "Please."

She bowed her head. "I wondered if you'd left."

She looked fragile and vulnerable. It made him want to hold her. He took a step closer. "I won't leave without saying good-bye. I swear it."

She turned then and looked at him curiously. "It was the press, wasn't it?"

He didn't say anything. He couldn't.

"Are you a criminal?"

He shook his head.

Her fine brows furrowed in confusion. "Is it something to do with your family?"

He let out a long sigh. "It's always something to do with my family."

"Well, I guess I can understand that."

She couldn't fathom the half of it, he thought, but she let him take her hand and walk beside her.

"Are you married?" she blurted out after a few steps.

He coughed to cover his amusement. "No."

"It's not funny, Al. You know much more about me than I know about you."

"Okay. I'm the oldest of four children. I'm thirty years old. I graduated from Oxford University. I'm on a monthlong vacation from a—job that's both draining and rewarding."

"A monthlong vacation in North Carolina?" she asked skeptically.

"Luck. Pure luck."

"Where were you born?" she ventured.

"At home," he sidestepped.

"And where is—"

He put his fingers over her mouth. "There are some answers I can't give you." A grim feeling came over him. "Later, but not now."

"That's a promise," Katherine whispered.

"Yes."

She took a deep breath. "One more question." She paused. "Are you promised to another woman?"

He thought of the relationship he'd just cut off. He thought, also, of the women his advisers would love to see him marry. "No."

She was cautious. "You had to think about it."

He took her other hand and made her face him. "I have neither publicly nor privately promised my love and life to another woman."

Tension coiled between them. It was always hovering. He saw it in her face, felt it in her grasp. "And now," he said in a low voice, "answer my question. Why are you out here in the rain?"

Katherine pulled back immediately. "Oh, no."

"I answered your questions."

She shook her head. "But this is, oh, this is craziness."

"We have a bargain," he reminded her.

She tried to pull away. "I can't say it to your face. It's too embarrassing."

He quickly solved that, pulling her into him. "Then say it to my chest."

Her groan vibrated against his ribs.

He waited, and when she didn't begin, he tried to help. "Was it the music again?"

She nodded, and he threaded his fingers through her damp hair. She huddled against him.

"And?"

Her sigh warmed a bare spot on his chest. "I had a dream."

He hugged her tighter, stroking her shoulders. "A nightmare?"

"No, but it was strange. You were in it, and you were wearing your mask. I tried to get it off, but I couldn't."

He was surprised, touched that such a small thing had distressed her. "Is that all?"

She burrowed her face into him farther, and his senses stirred. He noticed her feminine scent. He noticed she was braless. He noticed her belly rubbed against a rather sensitive part of his anatomy. And he also noticed that, for once, she wasn't trying to get away from him.

She cleared her throat. "You were touching me," she murmured. "Making love to me."

Alex's chest swelled. So she did dream of him. He kissed the top of her head. "Where were we?"

"In my bed. It was dark."

"Then how did you know it was me?"

"I knew."

His body immediately reacted. "Did I please you?"

"Yes," she admitted quietly.

His voice grew rough. "What did I do?"

She shook her head. "Al."

"Tell me."

"You kissed me and touched me, and"—her voice lowered to a whisper—"you said things."

"What things?"

"I don't remember," she said desperately.

"Katherine," Al began as he lifted her head. "Did I tell you that your eyes remind me of diamonds? That your laughter tugs and pulls at something inside me?"

Her lips trembled, and he kissed her. "How close did we get?"

"Very close."

"Was I inside you?"

She closed her eyes and spoke so softly that he barely heard her. "Yes."

The dam of his self-control broke. He kissed her again, intimately, in a way that showed her he wanted her. He ran his hands down her body, cupping her hips, lifting her against him. "Why do I feel like I've wanted you forever?" he murmured against her mouth, unable to stop touching her. "Why do I feel that if I don't taste you, I'll regret it for the rest of my life?"

"I don't know," Katherine murmured.

"Tell me you feel the same way." He kissed her a little roughly then. "Tell me you're not pretending."

"I do," she said, breathlessly. "I'm not pretending." Then she took a giant step farther and pushed aside his shirt and ran her hands over his chest.

Al shuddered. He snatched one of her hands and brought it to his lips, tasting his way from her fingertips down her arm to her shoulder.

Katherine instinctively arched her neck. He nuzzled her throat, murmuring dark, sexy words into her ear. Katherine was dizzy with him, his scent, his voice, him. At this moment it simply didn't matter that she didn't know as much about him as she wanted to.

He slid the strap of her sundress over one shoulder, and his hand followed the falling drape of material down her chest until the dress dangled on the beaded tip of her breast. "I dream of putting my mouth there," he said.

Her knees turned to putty. She looked into his dark, stormy eyes, and her breath caught. Slowly she exhaled, watching as he watched her dress fall to her waist. It was incredibly erotic to see his fascination with her breasts, to see him reach out and lightly touch and fondle. He plucked and fondled her nipples until she was biting back a moan. She rubbed her legs together, trying to assuage the restlessness that rushed through her.

"You are beautiful."

Al lifted her, wrapping her legs around his waist. She felt the measure of his arousal nudge at her, and a surge of fire licked through her veins.

He looked at her breasts and swollen nipples. He licked his lips. Then he looked into her eyes. "This is just the beginning."

SIX

If this was just the beginning, then she hoped he had a heart monitor handy.

"Oh!" Katherine gasped when his mouth found her breast. She slid her fingers through his hair, needing something to hold on to. He suckled her nipples until they were wet, stiff, and sensitive, and she felt the caress in her blood, his need in her heart.

Then he pulled back, the passion on his face so raw and basic, it made her burn. He looked at her, trailing his knuckles down her cheek. "Your breathing isn't quite so steady."

Al ran his finger around her mouth. She swallowed, then instinctively opened her lips wider. "Neither is yours." She darted out her tongue to taste his finger.

He sucked in a quick breath and nodded. "As you say." His gaze swept her again, and Katherine felt like a rich dessert served up for his pleasure. "I like the way your eyes glaze when I touch your breast. I like the way your breast tastes and feels in my mouth." He dropped his hand to one nipple and thumbed it in a lazy motion that made her thighs clench together.

He smiled then, like the devil. "I like the way you do that too." His lids lowered in sexy indolence. "I think I like everything about you, Katherine Kendall."

One of his hands slid up her thigh, beneath her panties, and squeezed. Her breath stopped.

"I just want more."

In a quick, smooth motion that left her more dizzy than before, Katherine found herself lying on the sand with him beside her. His hand slowly pulled the hem of her dress to her waist.

He toyed with the edge of her panties, brushing the backs of his fingers against her inner thigh. It was torment to have him so close to the place that ached. "Al," she pleaded.

"Shh," he said and continued, back and forth, moving closer and retreating, kissing her, slipping his tongue into her mouth. She was taunted and teased until she wondered if she'd remain in this state forever.

Until he finally touched her where she was moist and desperate. A moan broke from her throat. Her vision blurred. Her panties were discarded, and it seemed she felt him everywhere, her mouth and her cheek, her throat and breasts. And Katherine realized that although she'd been married, a man had never made love to her before.

He pulled away and looked down at her, breathing hard. His eyes were dark with passion. His hands rested on her inner thighs. "There's something else I want from you."

Katherine thought she knew what he was talking about, because she wanted the same thing. She wanted his closeness. She wanted nothing between them.

When he bent down and put his open mouth on her thigh, though, she jerked. He looked up and must have seen her shock. "Don't deny me this," he said in a rough, strained voice. "I can't leave without tasting you."

Her throat closed up. *Oh, my God.* She covered her face with a hand. The sight of his lips on her was unbearably erotic, but the sensation of them was torture. The journey he took was excruciatingly slow, his tongue skimming across her sensitized skin. Every nuance of movement danced through her system with arousing familiarity, the brush of his stubble, the controlled nip of his teeth. She'd heard his voice, rough with emotion, before. She'd inhaled his scent before. She'd done this before in her dreams. Her legs began to tremble.

She was totally under his power. Why did he

seem to know just how to touch and where? He could make her cry or laugh. He could make her shiver or moan. He could take her to the edge and leave her there, or push her over the edge. She hovered on that edge, undecided, vacillating, whether to stay or fly.

His mouth touched her intimately, sipping and stroking as if she were a tender bud ready to bloom. She was so swollen, she felt she was going to burst. She could barely breathe.

"Give me all of you, Katherine," he coaxed, his voice low. "All of you in my mouth." Then he touched her again. His tongue was tenderly persistent. His mouth was ruthlessly pleasure-giving.

Her blood roared through her veins as if it were jet-propelled. She arched off the ground, crying out his name. And her whole body convulsed into a chain of spasms within and without. One ended, and the next began, and the next.

And Katherine flew.

Moments later Alex was still trembling. He held Katherine in his arms. Or was it she who was holding him? For God's sake, why did he feel this way? After all, he had remained in control. He hadn't cried out. He hadn't come.

He'd thought to teach her, to show her how lovemaking could be. He hadn't counted on her teaching him that her sweet surrender would affect him like this.

He'd planned to bring her so much pleasure, she'd be crying with it. He hadn't planned on getting high from her complete responsiveness. He never would have believed the simple gesture of her hand on his cheek would render him speechless.

He'd planned to be the giver, yet he felt he was holding pure gold.

She stirred and pressed her face into his neck. Her breath fluttered in soft pants against his skin. His heart swelled within his chest, and he tightened his hold on her.

The mist still came down. The moon played peekaboo behind the clouds. The world was still spinning on its axis, he thought. So why did he feel completely undone?

Katherine stirred again and moved her mouth to his ear. "You can go ahead and say it," she whispered, the breathy sound tickling and arousing.

Alex's skin began to heat. "Say what?"

She continued nuzzling his throat. "I told you so."

It was difficult to concentrate with her hand skimming over his chest and down his belly. "I told you what?"

"That you would bring me incredible pleasure and that I would beg for it." She met his gaze a little shyly. "You were right."

Her fingers tugged at the top button of his pants. His blood pressure zoomed. "No," he choked out, reluctantly clutching her hand. "We can't. There's no protection." His full erection strained painfully against the tight pants. If he weren't a prince, Alex thought, he'd say to hell with it and finish what they'd started. But his father's indiscretions hung heavily over his head, making some actions impossible.

She lifted her head, looking at him uncertainly. "You don't want me to touch you."

"I didn't say that," Alex quickly corrected her. "I said—"

She covered his mouth with hers. He should stop her, he thought, as she unbuttoned his pants. He felt and heard the hiss of the zipper as she slowly lowered it.

She slid her hand under the edge of his briefs, and he groaned. She was so close. Maybe he could last for just a moment.

Her fingers grazed his masculinity. He ground his teeth.

"You're hard," she murmured.

"An understatement," he growled.

She brought her mouth an inch from his and murmured against his lips. "Next time, bring a condom."

Hell, he'd buy a whole factory.

When she wrapped her small but capable hand around him and stroked, he saw stars, and he knew there were none out tonight. He let out his breath in a long, uneven hiss.

Her thumb rubbed the tip, spreading a drop of his arousal and causing more. Just as he opened his mouth to tell her to stop, Katherine gave him a French kiss so erotic, there wasn't a rating for it. She slid her velvety tongue in and out of his mouth while she milked his throbbing shaft with her hand.

It was too much. She was too good. He couldn't stop. He jerked. He thrust, then spilled himself into her hand.

The hot, stinging release took his breath. Closing his eyes, he leaned his forehead against hers while he gathered his wits. Al shook his head. "Incredible," he muttered. "I haven't done this since—" He swore, then broke off.

"But I wanted you to," she said earnestly.

"Not that way. Not in your—" Lord, he felt like a fool, and he was supposed to be the experienced one.

"Yes, I did," she insisted in a husky voice. "It was—"

Curiosity got the better of him, and he looked at her closely. "It was what?"

She looked away, but not before he saw the intimate look on her face. "Sexy." She took a deep breath. "So sexy."

His body began to respond. Al groaned and kissed her. She opened her mouth to say something, but he shook his head. "Show some mercy, Katherine. Be quiet for a moment." Still oddly embarrassed, he stood and stripped off his pants. He pulled Katherine to her feet and lifted her dress, which was miraculously still on her, over her head.

She stared at him as if he'd gone crazy.

For once in his life Alex couldn't think of a single intelligent thing to say, so he just hauled her up in his arms and walked to the water's edge.

"What are we doing?"

"Going for a swim." He splashed through the waves until the ocean lapped against their lower bodies.

She tried to move away, but he wouldn't let her. "I thought you said we were going to swim."

Alex hugged her slippery, naked body to his. "I changed my mind."

"What if I want to swim?"

He looked as if he were going to overrule her, then he seemed to catch himself. "Do you wish to swim?"

"No." She smiled and shook her head ruefully. "I probably sound contrary, but you have this tendency to give orders that makes me feel like I'm supposed to click my heels and say, 'Yes sir!'"

He unbent and gave a half-grin. "Think of it as a genetic condition."

"*All* the men in your family are like this?"

Walking from the water, he nodded. "My father,

my grandfather, my great-grandfather, and on and on. Complete confidence is necessary for the job."

"You do the same work as your father, then?"

"Yes," he said in a tone that let her know he wouldn't explain further. He set her on the sand and pulled her dress over her head, then pulled on his pants. He took her hand. "It's late, *chérie*. We should go back now."

They walked in silence, and as they neared the cottage, Katherine thought of what they'd done and what they hadn't. Suddenly she couldn't accept not knowing about him. Too much had happened between them. Or had it just happened to her?

"You're thinking too much," Al said.

"Maybe. But you're quiet too. What are you thinking?"

Al stopped outside the door and brushed a stray strand of hair from her forehead. "That you're going to scowl at me in the morning if you don't get some sleep."

So he wanted it light and easy, she thought with a twist in her stomach. She wasn't sure she could manage it, but she took a deep breath and mustered a smile. "Good night, then."

She glanced away, then felt his hand on her shoulder. "Tonight, *mon amie*, there are no right words."

She looked into his dark eyes and saw the glimmer of something deeper. Her heart bumped along unsteadily. Declarations and promises whirled in her head, frightening her with their strength. She was connected to him, yet somehow not.

"You're right," she whispered. "Everything is either too little or too much." She reached up and kissed the corner of his mouth. "Till tomorrow."

He clutched her waist possessively and kissed her full on the mouth, obliterating his earlier light tone. "Dream of me," he muttered, then urged her through the door.

The next morning Alex rose before Katherine and Chad. He felt like a new man, young and free. The crunchy horrible coffee he made couldn't even dim his grin.

He tossed it out and traded it for a glass of orange juice, then strolled onto the front porch. The sun was just rising. He breathed in the salty morning air.

He caught sight of a paper bag on the bottom step. He picked it up and opened it. The silky triangle of Katherine's panties was the only item it held.

His stomach turned at the realization of what it meant.

Someone had watched them. Someone had watched what should have been private. Someone had watched her nearly naked and needy beneath him.

Fury shot through him, nearly blinding him with the force of it. He crumpled the bag and cursed, scanning the wooded area, suddenly knowing he wasn't alone. "Show yourself," he called in a rigid, quiet voice.

A man immediately stepped forward. Dressed like the other campers, he wore jeans and a T-shirt, but Alex stiffened. He knew him. "Who sent you?"

"Isabella."

He would tear out her hair when he saw her. "How many others?"

"One. He sleeps."

Alex's jaw clenched. "You will speak of this to no one."

"Of course."

The man was sworn to protect and defend Alex at all costs. He was also sworn to secrecy. "Jean-Luc, in two weeks I return to Moreno. Until then, keep your distance."

Jean-Luc nodded. "Yes, Your Highness."

"Al Sanders," Alex corrected. "No one must know."

Jean-Luc looked uncomfortable. With great reluctance, he nodded again. "Yes—" He hesitated. "Al." Then he disappeared into the woods.

Alex rubbed the back of his neck in frustration. He probably shouldn't have been so hard on the man. Jean-Luc was only trying to do his job, and the bag was a pointed reminder of the penalties of being indiscreet. Princes didn't make love with women on public beaches. Anyone could have been watching.

A reporter would have a field day with this kind of story, Alex thought. Where had his mind been, to put Katherine and himself in such a compromising situation?

He heard the squeak of the screen door and quickly turned. Fresh from a shower, Katherine stood there with a soft smile on her face. "Good morning."

Torn by self-condemnation and the effect her morning-husky voice had on his system, he nodded stiffly. "How are you?"

Katherine's smile wavered at his cool tone. "I, uh, I'm a little tired."

"Yes. I regret I kept you out so late."

"Regret?" The word deflated her. She looked at him carefully, noting the rigid set of his jaw, the stoic expression on his face, and the unhappiness in his eyes. She couldn't help but recall other morning-afters when she'd hoped for warmth and love and gotten neither. Her heart sank. Perhaps, she thought with a bitter taste in her mouth, she'd mis-read his feelings.

Regret. What a horrible word to use to describe such a beautiful evening. He couldn't have meant it. She took a deep breath. "You regret last night."

"I didn't mean it that way," he said quickly in a harsh voice. "This morning I realized we weren't discreet. Anyone could have seen us."

Relief trickled through her, and she smiled tentatively. He'd been worried about privacy. "But no one did, Al." She reached out a hand to reassure him.

He backed away.

The bottom seemed to fall out of her stomach, and she dropped her hand to her side. She felt she was in the middle of her worst nightmare. "You don't want me to touch you," she whispered.

"It's not that," he said. Chad's cheery whistle carried from the kitchen. Al looked at Katherine's face and knew he would have to tell her who he was. But now was not the time. "We'll talk later."

End of discussion. She'd heard the tone before. Temper warred with pain. "Don't count on it."

He swore under his breath. "You'll get all your answers later. Now is not the time." Then he walked away.

Katherine stared after him for a full moment. A full moment praying he'd turn around, tell her he'd been wrong and that he'd dreamed of her.

He didn't, and the feeling of loss crushed her. She clasped her trembling hands together.

She felt like a fool. The pain was so bad, her chest hurt with it. Her face ached. Her eyes throbbed. She felt like throwing up.

She was hurt, and she hated herself for it. She'd been ready to make Al's breakfast and coo over him like a lovesick idiot. Her cheeks burned with humiliation. Thank goodness she hadn't gotten that far.

The shame was too much. It cut too close to older wounds.

She slammed the screen door and stomped into the kitchen. She crammed a slice of bread into the toaster.

"Hey, Katie," Chad said, "give the toaster a break. It's pretty old. And you know," he chided, his mouth full of sugar-coated cereal, "Napoléon made coffee again. You're supposed to stay on top of that. Next time he might ruin the coffeemaker."

"If you want coffee, then make it yourself."

Chad's eyes widened. "Well, excuuuuse me. What burr have you got in your craw?"

"Maybe I'm just not feeling very cheerful this morning, Chad. Maybe it would be best if you didn't talk to me."

"Well, you better find your charm. Some guy named Jeff Windsor called and said he wanted to tour the campground today." He took a gulp of milk and stared at her. "You wanna tell me what's going on?"

"Not really."

"Are you trying to find a buyer for Uncle Jasper?"

She couldn't evade his direct question. "Yes, but the final decision will be his. I'm just trying to make it easier."

Chad stopped eating and looked at her. "He may not thank you, Katie."

She ran a hand through her hair. "I know, but I've got to try." Lord, what a day. First Al, now this. "You won't tell Jasper, will you?"

He shook his head. "Nah. He doesn't call that much anyway." He stirred his cereal. "I'm gonna miss it if I have to leave, though."

Her heart twisted. She understood why he wanted some stability in his life. He'd had so little. "Maybe we can work it out for you to stay on."

Chad shrugged. "Maybe. Maybe not. You gonna tell me what's going on between you and Napoléon?"

This one was easy. Determination surged through her. "Nothing. Absolutely nothing."

Katherine slapped on some emotional Band-Aids, dusted off her pride, and met Jeff Windsor. She'd prepared herself for another crusty whiner like Mr. Logan. Jeff Windsor, however, was a surprise. For one thing he was younger and more attractive than her other prospect.

"The campground isn't in perfect condition," she warned him honestly.

Jeff smiled. "Nothing's perfect." He gave her an appreciative glance and an exaggerated wink. "With all due respect, though, you come pretty close."

It was such an audacious comment that she laughed. She spent the day with him and lapped up his harmless, uninhibited flirting as if it were whipped cream on top of a sundae.

Jeff's sense of humor and easy smile were a balm to her injured soul. A few times throughout the day she felt Al's dark gaze on her. Thoughts of him distracted her, tugged at her, but she threw them off.

"I've monopolized every minute of your day," Jeff said, looking at his watch. "But I'd appreciate your sharing dinner with me if you think you can bear my presence a little longer."

Katherine gave a long-suffering sigh. "It'll be a stretch," she teased, "but I think I'm up to it. Let me go wash up. Is the grill okay?"

Jeff nodded. "Fifteen minutes."

Humming, she skipped to the cottage and ran up the steps. She pulled open the door and walked straight into Al's hard chest.

"Oh!" She stumbled backward, her pulse jumping. "Excuse me." She shifted to go around him.

He shifted too.

She took a deep breath and tried again. "Excuse me."

Al matched her step for step.

She set her mouth and looked at him. "I need to wash for dinner."

"It's time to talk," he said in a low voice.

The same low voice he'd used last night, Katherine realized. She wasn't immune to it, but she shook her head. "I can't. I'm meeting a prospective buyer for dinner."

"The man you've been with today."

Something about his tone set her teeth on edge. "The man I've been showing around the camping resort today," she corrected.

He nodded shortly. "Then I'll join you. You need someone with you to protect your interests."

Taken aback, Katherine gaped at him. "No," she finally managed, torn between surprise and anger. "Jeff Windsor is a perfect gentleman. He treats me with respect. I can handle this just fine."

She sensed his frustration and something else. He looked trapped and burdened. It was probably a guilty conscience because he'd acted like a bastard this morning. Well, her ego couldn't take another beating, and she didn't want to hear a bunch of lame apologies, so she did something she wasn't particularly good at. She lied.

"Listen, Al, it's okay. You don't have to explain anything to me." She stopped looking at him and started talking faster. "I've had time to think about it, and I probably just made a big deal out of something that wasn't such a big deal to you. Last night we didn't do anything irrevocable. Some people would just call it heavy petting." She shrugged, thinking she was spouting the biggest boatload of brown stuff she'd ever heard come out of her mouth.

"We're fortunate that you had the good sense to

stop so there wouldn't be any long-lasting conse—"

He caught her shoulders. "You can't mean this."

His gaze was turbulent and full of pain. Katherine closed her eyes against it. "Oh, Al, don't do this to me. It's not fair. I'm not sophisticated and worldly. I may have a strong backbone, but I've got thin skin. If you've got an ounce of kindness in you, then leave me alone." She met his gaze. "I can't handle this hot-and-cold stuff."

"I didn't explain myself well this morning," he said. "Last night was important to me too. And,"—he looked at the ceiling—"if I were anyone but who I am, I wouldn't have stopped."

"You're not making any sense."

"Yes, I am." He looked as if he were searching for the right words. "This morning I couldn't wait to see you, to touch you again, to see if you were real."

It was what she'd wanted to hear. This morning. "Al, you moved away when I tried to touch you," she reminded him.

He frowned. "That was after . . ."

"After what?"

He released her and ran a hand through his hair. "After I saw someone who reminded me of my position and my responsibilities."

Katherine was completely confused. "*Who* in the world did you see?"

Al placed his hands on his hips, and his lip

twitched in dissatisfaction. "One of my body-guards."

"Bodyguard," she echoed. Her heart thumped in trepidation. Why did Al need a bodyguard? More than one bodyguard.

"Jean-Luc must have witnessed"—he threw out his hand in a gesture of frustration—"us last night. He found your panties and left them in a bag on the front porch."

Katherine's eyes rounded in shock. She'd been so overwhelmed by Al and the passion of the moment that she could have barely recalled her name last night, let alone a pair of panties. She cringed in embarrassment. "Oh, my God. Someone did watch us."

"I felt the same way. If it helps, Jean-Luc will never speak of it."

She felt a blush spread from her toes to the top of her head. "He won't have to. Just knowing—" She covered her cheeks with her hands.

He covered her hands with his and shook his head. "There is no shame in what we did, *chérie*."

Her heart dipped at the naked look in his eyes. "Now you understand why I acted the way I did this morning."

Katherine's head reeled with everything he said. She squinted her eyes together trying to sort it all out. She understood he hated the fact that they'd been watched. She understood he'd been upset and acted remote. She still, however, had no idea why his bodyguards were here. Fresh out of clues and patience, she shook her head. "Al, just who the hell are you?"

He sighed and moved her hands from her cheeks to the space between them, twining his fingers with hers. She wondered if he was making sure she wouldn't run. The longer he waited, the more nervous she got. It can't be that bad, she told herself.

"It can't be that bad," she repeated out loud.

He gave her a half-smile. "Some days it's not." Then he grew serious again. "I'm not sure how to explain this."

Katherine was going nuts. She rolled her eyes. "Start with something basic. You name. Is Al Sanders your real name?"

He shook his head, and Katherine told herself as long as he didn't say he was Elvis or the Antichrist, it would be okay.

"My name is Prince Alexander Ferdinand Merrick de Moreno."

SEVEN

"Elvis" would have been better.

Katherine's jaw dropped down to her chest. Her knees lost their starch, and it was one heck of a good thing that Al was holding her up.

Her mind started to function again, and she shook her head. A prince on Pirate Island? Al must be deluding himself, she thought, because it simply wasn't possible. It was painful to admit, but the man was a couple of cookies short of a dozen. He was crazy. Sexy, but crazy. She felt a surge of sympathy.

"Al," she began, smiling gently and pulling her hands from his, "is there any sort of medication you're supposed to be taking?"

Al looked puzzled. "Medication?"

Katherine nodded. "Yes. Something a doctor may have prescribed for you." She waved her hand. "Perhaps for your head."

"I rarely get headaches."

"Yes, but—" She was at a loss. "There are effective medications for confusion and depression and mood swings."

"Since I'm not confused or depressed, I don't have a need for those medications."

She remained silent, unable to keep the pity and disbelief from her face.

It took him a minute, then the clouds cleared away. He chuckled. "You don't believe me!"

"Now, Al," she began in a soothing tone.

He couldn't contain his mirth. "Would papers help?" He continued laughing.

His helpless laughter was getting on her nerves. "Papers can be forged," she said primly.

Al hooted, losing all semblance of dignity. "I could always get my bodyguard to identify me."

Katherine frowned at the man holding his stomach and laughing without restraint. "Al, this is serious. If you have a mental problem, you need to get medical attention."

"Mental problem?" His chuckles gradually subsided into occasional spurts of laughter. Finally he gave a long sigh. "Okay, I'll supply some evidence." He extended his hand. "Have you ever noticed my ring?"

Katherine looked at the elaborately engraved gold ring and shrugged. "I just assumed it was a fraternity ring."

"Look again," he said. "It's my country's seal. The translation for the words is 'Merrick, Ruler of Moreno. Forever.'"

A shiver ran through her. Still, she found it difficult to accept. "I've never heard of Moreno."

"It's a small country in the Mediterranean. We export spices, and tourism is growing every year. We're probably best known for our annual fencing tournaments, although most of our visitors are from Europe. The Americans tend to stick to the French Riviera."

Hanging on to her skepticism, she cocked her head to one side. "Where do you live?"

He shrugged. "In the palace. It's not," he said in response to her unspoken question, "as glamorous as it seems. The original structure is over two hundred years old, and it seems to be in a constant state of renovation."

"Sort of like our state highways," she murmured. Bits and pieces of their conversations nudged at her. The gears of her mind shifted slowly, grinding and dragging with the effort. It all started to make sense. Al's fencing skill. His natural tendency to lead and, she grimaced, often give orders. His fine clothing when he first arrived. His inability to make coffee.

She looked at him and suddenly felt out of her depth. He was a man, yet somehow much more. She could easily imagine him wearing a fine robe and a crown on his head. She could easily imagine him dressed in a stunning formal uniform at a ball, waltzing with a beautiful woman.

She could not easily imagine the woman being her.

He stepped close to her, his gaze intent. "Don't pull back now."

Her pulse picked up. "I don't know what to say." She lifted her shoulders. "I don't know what to call you."

He lifted her hand and brushed the back of it with a kiss. "When we're alone, call me Alex."

She felt her skin burn. "I'm not sure being alone is a good idea. How do we know when we're really alone?"

He shook his head. "Don't think of it. For the rest of my time here the guards will keep their distance. They won't intrude."

Her heart dropped to her stomach. *For the rest of my time here.* It stuck like a scratched record, playing over and over in her mind. She looked at him again. So, what was she to him? An amusement? That stung.

For that matter what was he to her? The implications of that question troubled her. It shouldn't matter what he was to her, because he was leaving. She'd always known that. So why did it hurt?

Once he left, she'd never see him again. She didn't move in his circles, never would.

"You're quiet," he said.

She pushed back her hair and turned away from his questioning eyes. "I'm thinking."

"God forbid," he muttered.

She shot him a reproving glance. "It's a lot to take in, Al—Alex. It changes things."

"No, it doesn't," he insisted, full of determination. "Not for the next two weeks."

She sighed in exasperation. "Yes, it does," she argued. "For Pete's sake, you live in a palace, you have bodyguards. Someday you'll rule a country. You are not an ordinary man."

He swung her around to face him. "Yes, I am, damnit!" His eyes flashed with anger. "And after last night, if anyone knows that I'm a mere mortal man, it should be you."

She felt the heat of his emotions. He was so full of masculine passion, anger, and pain, she felt it in every crevice of her mind and heart. It was too powerful, too potent for her to handle. At a loss, she took a step back.

"Katherine," a voice called from the door. "Are we still on for dinner?"

Katherine darted a quick glance at the door and winced. "Oh, no! It's Jeff. I completely forgot. Be there in a minute," she called, then turned back to Alex with a look of distress.

Alex fought the urge to make her stay, make her accept him and everything he was. The instinct to slam the door in Jeff's face was overwhelming. Nothing had been settled between them, and Alex could feel her slipping away. "We need to finish this," he said in a low voice. "You need to see that nothing is changed."

"Oh, Alex." Her eyes were sad and confused. "I don't know if that's possible."

He refused to believe it. "We'll talk after you get back. I'll wait."

She shook her head slowly. "Don't," she whispered, then turned and left.

Katherine looked out the window at the downpour and flashes of lightning.

"Is it always this rainy?" Jeff asked.

"This summer's a little wetter than usual." She glanced at him and tried for a smile. "It hasn't affected business, though, if that's what you're asking."

He paused, then nodded in the direction of her plate. "Full?"

Katherine felt the strain of keeping her lips curved upward. "Yes," she said, thinking that was exactly how she felt. Not full of food, but full of confusion and shock. So full she didn't feel like smiling or talking. The idea of eating the rest of her hamburger made her stomach turn. She thought of Alex and what he was. A prince. Another politician, she thought, and shook her head at what a lousy joke fate had played on her.

"Earth to Katherine, come in please," Jeff said. "I asked that last question three times. Where are you?"

"Oh!" She winced, chagrined. "I'm sorry."

He gave a wry smile. "I guess I'm not riveting company this evening."

"Oh, no," she protested, feeling guilty. "It's not you. It's me. I'm the one who's not riveting. Now what was that question?"

"I wondered how often you get to the mainland. I'd like to take you to dinner some time."

She couldn't be less interested, and wanted to kick herself for feeling that way. "I'm so busy with the—" She stopped as the dining-hall door flew open, and Chad burst in, wet and panicky.

He rushed to her side. "We've got a problem. Georgia Hawkins said Davy's missing. She's been looking for him for an hour. She turned her back, and he just disappeared."

Alarm shot through Katherine. "But he's only three. Where could he have gone?"

Chad shook his head helplessly. "Who knows? She checked all the community rooms. I checked the bathrooms and showers. Al is searching the woods."

"Al?" A loud boom of thunder split the air. Katherine thought of the heavily wooded acres on the edge of the campground property and shuddered. "That's a horrible place to be during a storm."

"Yeah, listen, you'd better look in on Georgia. She's getting all upset."

Another sharp crack of thunder echoed through the room. "Where are you going?"

Chad shrugged as if the choice were obvious. "To the woods." Then he hurried to the door.

"Be careful," Katherine called. She turned to Jeff, rising at the same time. "I'm sorry, but I really must leave. If you have any other questions, just call." She lifted her palms. "I guess I didn't do a great sales job."

Jeff waved her off. "Don't worry. I'll call."

Katherine headed for Georgia Hawkins's tent.

A long sixty minutes later Katherine brought Georgia to the cottage and fixed her a cup of herbal tea. The woman was in tears. "It's like he vanished," she said in a wobbly voice. "My husband left six months ago, and I've had to work such long hours. I thought Davy would love a camping trip."

"I'm sure he has," Katherine said soothingly, keeping one eye on the time. *Where was Alex?*

"But—"

The door flew open, and Alex strode in with Davy, drenched and crying, in his arms. Chad and three other men came in behind them.

"Davy!" Georgia rushed to take the little boy in her arms.

"He's got a few scratches," Alex told her, handing over the little boy. "He was in the woods and got scared when lightning struck a tree and knocked it down."

"Oh, thank you," Georgia whispered. "This has been the longest night of my life."

Fifteen minutes later Georgia and Davy left to spend the night in a cabin. Katherine sent along milk and cookies, but Davy was asleep before Georgia said her last thank-you. The three other men followed Georgia out the door, and Chad raided the kitchen.

Al and Katherine stood silently facing each other in the den. After the din of anxious, excited voices, the room seemed painfully quiet. The tension between them was thick and awkward. She searched for something to say, noticing the scrapes on his arms and face.

"Davy wasn't the only one who got scratched," she finally blurted out.

Al rubbed a mark on his cheek. "He was hiding in some berry bushes. They had thorns."

Katherine felt a trickle of relief. As a first-grade teacher, she felt scratches and scrapes were her domain. She was glad to have something to do instead of staring at him like a tongue-tied idiot. "You'll need some antibiotic cream on those scrapes so they won't get infected," she said briskly. "Wait right there, and I'll get it."

"Is that an order?" he asked in a mild voice.

She narrowed her eyes, trying to see what his mood was, but his face was blank of expression. "Yes, it is. Have a seat, Your Highness."

She heard his muttered curse as she turned, and didn't have to wonder about his mood anymore. Royally nasty, she thought, and grinned at her private joke. She dampened a washcloth with warm water, collected the cream and Band-Aids from the medicine cabinet, and returned to find him on the sofa with a dark expression on his face.

Sitting beside him, she immediately decided there was a huge difference between caring for a first grader's scrapes and caring for Al's. She considered leaving the first-aid paraphernalia with him and retreating, but her conscience got the best of her. She squared her shoulders. "Hands first."

He extended his right one, and she winced at the damage. "This must have hurt. Why didn't you mention it when you first came in?"

"It's just blood, Katherine. All men bleed, even me."

Her gaze shot up to meet his, and the silence hung between them, again, this time more charged than before. She bit her lip.

She gently cleaned his hand, feeling its warmth and strength beneath hers, remembering the tenderness in his touch. The quiet allowed her to think of things best forgotten, to hear the melody that had become his theme song in her heart. She fought against it. "The washcloth might burn a little bit," she said, her voice sounding loud, "but the cream won't hurt."

She looked at his arms and remembered how they felt wrapped around her. His skin was smooth, but he was hard beneath. She wondered about his heart. Was it hard too? Was it jaded? Was it capable of love? Damn. The back of her neck grew warm, and she began to feel edgy. "Need a drink?" she asked, abruptly standing. "We've probably got something around here. What's your pleasure?"

He looked at her in that dark, intent way of his. It was annoying because it made her feel exposed. It made her heart jump and her mouth go dry as sand. It made her wish like hell he'd hurry up and answer.

"What do you have?"

Katherine turned to the cabinet where her uncle kept his liquor and began pulling out the bottles. "I don't know. Vodka, Caribbean rum, gin, scotch." She stopped. "I guess that's it."

"Scotch, neat."

"Okay," she said, splattering some of the liquid into a glass. In deference to her nerves she poured some into another glass and took a gulp. The bitter liquid nearly scalded her throat. She wheezed and made a face.

"Not your poison?" Al asked in dry tones.

"No. I'd just as soon keep my vocal cords intact."

Deliberately avoiding his gaze, Katherine gave Al's glass to him and started with his other hand, working quickly. She hummed "The Twelve Days of Christmas" in her mind and planned what color nail polish she'd put on tonight.

After a few minutes she took a deep breath and turned to Al's face. She could have used another drink now. She looked into his eyes and almost moaned. *Make that two drinks.*

Al broke the silence. "You asked what was my pleasure."

She bit her lip and counted the remaining scrapes—five. If she worked fast, maybe—

"Shall I tell you what I really want?"

"I can guess." Her voice was squeaky. Three more to go, she thought desperately.

"It would be my pleasure to take you to bed and spill a glass of wine over your body, then sip up every drop."

Katherine swallowed. "Alex—"

"The next glass would be your chance to return the favor."

Katherine's mouth went dry. She was suddenly shamefully thirsty.

"After we'd driven each other completely crazy with our mouths, I'd pull you on top of me and slowly push my way in where you're wet and ready for me." He lifted her hand to his mouth and branded her with a quick dart of his tongue. "Are you wet and ready now?"

"No!" she lied, jerking her hand from his. "No, damnit, no." Tears of frustration, sexual and emotional, burned her eyes like fire. She stumbled backward, feeling raw and vulnerable. "Why are you doing this?" she whispered.

He stood, and his face showed some of the torment she felt. That only made it worse.

"Because you need to see," he said in a low, urgent voice, "that like any other man, I bleed and want. Like any other man, I can need so much it hurts."

Katherine shook her head. She couldn't deal with the intensity of him. He was so powerful, she worried she might lose herself in him and never find her way out. She shook her head, torn between terror and want. "I can't be what you need. It's too much." Her voice broke. "I'm not enough. And there'd be nothing left of me. I'm sorry."

"How can you not be enough when you're more than I've ever had before?"

Her chest tightened painfully.

He stepped forward and cupped her jaw in his hand. The tenderness stalled her movement.

"I've hurt you again, *chérie*, when I only want to make you happy." He gave an ironic smile. "If I can't have you tonight in my bed, I'll have you in my dreams. Say you'll dream of me."

Katherine squeezed her eyes and breathed in his scent. The music played again. Her throat hurt. "That's easy," she said huskily. "I always dream of you." She kissed his palm. He sucked in a deep breath, and she felt cheated. She wanted the wine and his naked body and the taste of his passion. Katherine opened her eyes and felt his smoldering desire wrap around her like a velvet chain.

She jerked free and walked away, one foot in front of the other until she stood in her room. Her neatly made bed mocked her. Katherine flipped on both lights and turned on her radio. She pulled out her fingernail polish. "I'm gonna have the best damn nails in the Western Hemisphere," she muttered to herself as she unscrewed the top of Passion-Fruit Plum.

He just wants two weeks. Just two weeks. The words played in her head over the next two days, nudging her, tormenting her. A superficial truce seemed to have been called between them. Alex didn't touch her. He didn't make any more heated comments about his desire for her. But his eyes did. The restlessness and wanting were always there ready to explode.

The wanting was the worst. It was almost a visible force, with her every minute, a threat and an invitation. She couldn't escape it in her sleep. The last two nights, she'd heard him stop outside her bedroom door. She held her breath, and an eternity passed before he walked on to his room. He hadn't said a word, but she'd felt his call. In the middle of the night she woke, reaching for him, and feeling foolish when she heard herself murmur his name out loud.

She was sitting right on the edge, and the only thing that kept her from going over was the fact that her emotions went far deeper than a two-week romp in bed. She cared about him. She cared about what went on inside him, what he had to hide because of who he was.

The oddest development in all this, Katherine thought, was the way Chad had begun including Alex in his daily activities. Their joint search for Davy must have forged a link between them.

They had spent most of yesterday taking a chain saw to the fallen tree in the woods. After dinner they disappeared with a couple of six-packs of beer. She'd later found them smoking cigars and playing a cut-throat poker game *in her office*.

Too stunned to chew them out, she'd told them to clean up before they left. She'd lay odds Chad was teaching Alex everything he knew about cheating. Her brother was corrupting him.

Katherine frowned, looking at her alarm clock. Twelve o'clock. There'd been talk of a coon hunt tonight, murmurs about Chuck's Bar.

She punched her pillow and turned over, refusing to think about it one second longer. At this rate she'd use up all her nail polish in one week. Alex had bodyguards to protect him against any mischief Chad might dream up.

She'd barely drifted off when a loud noise woke her. She sat up, clutching the front of her gown. Someone was singing. She cocked her head to the side, listening. Her eyes widened in surprise. Make that two male someones.

". . . dead skunk in the middle of the road," they loudly chorused together, a mile off key.

"Great," she muttered, snatching her robe and thrusting her arms through the sleeves. "This is just great." She pushed her hair out of her face and stomped into the hallway.

Leaning on Chad, Alex started bellowing out lines from "Your Cheatin' Heart."

"Stop it! Stop it!" Katherine glared at her brother and Alex. "You'll wake the guests, and I'll have to explain why I have two lunatics in my house."

"Aw, Katie," Chad began, stumbling forward.

Katherine stepped back. "Don't you 'Aw, Katie' me. You're drunk, and look what you've done to Al. He can barely stand."

"I'm in full control of my faculties, Katherine. I'm never drunk." He swayed.

Katherine rolled her eyes. "I'm not sure I want to know, but where have you been?"

"Chuck's," Alex said. His lips twitched. "The whiskey was better this time."

Chad started laughing. "That's cause you weren't wearing it." He slapped Alex on the back.

When they started up the chorus of another song, Katherine groaned.

"Go to bed," she said over the noise. She pushed Chad toward his bedroom. "You'll be worthless in the morning."

"But, Katie—"

"Go," she said firmly, wondering how Chad would feel about being responsible for causing an international incident. He reluctantly meandered away, alternately humming and laughing.

Turning to Alex, Katherine took a deep breath, inhaling the scent of whiskey and overpowering perfume. She gritted her teeth. God help her, the man was sexy even when he was drunk. His hair was attractively mussed. His shirt was unbuttoned nearly to his waist.

She wondered how many female hands had caressed his chest tonight. A swift surge of jealousy took the bottom out of her stomach.

"You look angry," he said.

"How can you tell? You're drunk."

"Not really." He leaned closer and lowered his voice. "Princes don't get drunk."

Katherine sighed. "I can't believe you did this. What if someone from the press had seen you?"

He shrugged his broad shoulders. She bit back a moan. Even his shrug was sexy.

"I'd tell them a woman had driven me to it. A siren redhead plucked my heart and 'stomped that sucker flat,'" he quoted in round, cultured tones.

She smothered a laugh. "Go to bed."

"Come with me."

Her breath caught. "No."

"Then let me sleep with you."

Katherine swallowed, shaking her head. "You need to get some rest, Alex. You'll feel better in the morning." What a crock, she thought. He was going to feel terrible in the morning.

He leaned closer. "I don't want to sleep without you tonight."

Katherine caught sight of something on his ear and lost the thread of the conversation. It glinted in the light. She blinked, then gasped. "You've got an earring!"

"It's a stud," he corrected her. "It has some sort of sexual connotation in your country. Lucy said—"

"Lucy," she repeated in a deadly voice. "Just what is your relationship with Lucy?"

For a moment Alex actually looked flustered. Katherine was torn between amazement and feminine pique.

"It's not what you think. She pierced my ear and offered—"

"Pierced!" she shrieked. "You mean this isn't temporary?" She was furious. This woman had violated Alex. She'd stuck a needle in his ear. Katherine narrowed her eyes. "I'll just bet she offered you plenty."

"You're not listening. She offered me some advice on how to win you over."

Katherine didn't believe it. Not for one minute. "And did she demonstrate?" she asked sweetly.

"No," he said in a blunt voice. "A few others tried. You want me to name them?"

She saw the menace on his face and ignored it. The idea of another woman's hands on him made her crazy. "I'm sure it would take all night," she hissed back at him.

"You may be right." He took her by the shoulders, and she felt the strength of his grip, heard the frustrated power in his voice. Too late, she realized he was past reason.

"I want *you* right now." His voice was rough. "Do you understand? No preliminaries. No romantic words. I want to put you against that wall, lift your gown. And to hell with who I am, I just want inside where you're hot and slippery for me."

It should have sounded crude, but the same wanting pulsed inside her with every beat of her heart. He wanted her, desperately. And she wanted, desperately, to know him as intimately as possible.

"Are you scared? If you're not, then you should be," he bit out, holding her gaze. "Because I'm three seconds away from following through on my words."

When she didn't move, his eyelids lowered. "One."

Katherine swallowed.

"Two," he said harshly.

She closed her eyes. Where was her sense? She should be running—alone—back to her room.

"Three."

She could almost hear the click of a locked door. No going back. She'd made her choice. She licked her lips.

He took a deep breath. Katherine opened her eyes to find him staring at her, unvarnished need on his face. His hand slid to her hips, and he lifted her gown.

EIGHT

Katherine's heart thumped wildly in her chest. She flexed her fingers on his shoulders, remembering that Chad was just down the hall. She suddenly felt self-conscious. "Could we do this behind closed doors this time?" she whispered. "I'd really like it to be just you and me."

Alex didn't say anything, just swung her up in his arms and walked into his bedroom. He shut the bedroom door with his foot. Before her feet touched the floor, he was lifting the gown over her head and pushing her panties down her trembling legs. He muttered something dark in French, then kissed her, his tongue thrusting into her mouth. His hands were everywhere, heating her skin, thumbing her nipples, tracing the curve of her waist.

Just as he promised, there were no preliminaries. But Katherine could feel his wild heartbeat against her. She could see the need on his face; and the desperation behind his every movement was the biggest turn-on she'd ever had.

He squeezed her hips, then tested the dampness between her legs with fingers that probed and stroked. "Unbutton my shirt," he said in a low, husky voice, continuing the sweet assault on her. "God, I can't keep my hands off you."

The intimate caress made her weak. With shaking fingers she rid him of the shirt. She savored the rough texture of his chest with her hands. Bowing her head against the solid muscular wall, she rubbed her cheek against it, absorbing his heat. Then touching and breathing weren't enough, and she darted her tongue out to taste him.

He jerked. She felt his breath stop, and something deep inside her bloomed, making her bold. Katherine eased her hands down his belly to his bulging erection and cupped him through his jeans. "I want all of you this time, Alex," she whispered in a voice she nearly didn't recognize as her own. "Everything you've got to give me."

His eyes flared with black fire, and within a heartbeat she was on her back with the cool comforter beneath her. She watched his face, taut with urgency, as he slid down his zipper. The grating sound tickled her nerve endings like a velvet whip. And that earring taunted her with its wickedness.

He shoved his pants down, revealing his erection, thick and full. Her breath grew shallow. The air was filled with the scent of musk and need. She stared at him, and a primitive thrill shot through her.

In turn, his gaze fell over her as if he were a starving man given his first meal. Katherine did nothing to hide her intense desire. She wanted him to see. She wanted him to feel. Her nipples tightened. Her belly rippled. She rubbed her thighs together to soothe the restlessness inside her.

Alex saw it all and grew thick with need. "I want everything at once," he whispered harshly. "How do you do this to me?"

Katherine took a quick breath. The tiniest sliver of age-old feminine fear edged in, oddly increasing her excitement to fever pitch.

"Wider," he murmured, pushing her thighs apart. The secrets of her femininity lay bare in front of him; the sweet scent of her arousal filled his head. He rubbed one finger down the center of her, circling the exposed bead, then plunging into her glistening moistness.

She arched against him, reaching for him. "I want to touch you." He moved slightly to grant her access, and her hands slipped around him, adoring him with her touch.

Her caresses spent his control. It was suddenly too much. After slipping on protection, he positioned himself at her moist entrance. Then, in one smooth, fluid movement, he thrust all the way into her.

Her breath caught and shattered.

His own breath coming hard and fast, he hesitated, watching her. "Did I hurt you?"

She shook her head, spilling her silky hair from side to side. "No." Her face was open and wanton. "But I need you closer," she said in a voice that hitched with emotion. "Please hold me?"

Alex's heart took a free-fall. He lowered himself to her, feeling the delicious stab of her nipples against his chest, then he wrapped his hands beneath her, resting his weight on his elbows so that he wouldn't crush her. "Is this what you want?"

"For starters." She kissed his neck and slid her fingers through his hair.

Her sweet affection undid him. Her body squeezed his like a tight, hot glove. The pleasure was so intense, it was almost painful. He ground his teeth together. Lost in the clench of her sweet inner walls, he was overwhelmed by the need for release. But he fought it because he wanted it all for both of them.

Katherine rocked beneath him, sensing his reticence. Even in the midst of his need, she felt the tenderness in his restraint, and it brought tears to her eyes. But the sensation of his fullness rubbing inside was like a hot wire against her nerve endings. He would give her what she needed. She was sure of it. The certainty gave her the freedom to take.

She reached her hands down between them and

pulled back enough to rub the length of him before he entered her again and again.

"Oh, my God," he muttered hoarsely.

She kissed him, an openmouthed invitation that he took. Every movement was pulling at her, dragging her closer. Every shift gave a breathtaking hint of mindless ecstasy that seemed to grow with each second. She shuddered and clutched his shoulders for strength, losing herself with each thrust of his tongue and each pumping caress from his manhood.

He mastered her mouth and her body until she was weeping with it. He murmured brokenly in French, and her arousal gushed through her like a tidal wave, a solid wall of incredible pleasure that took her past the point of return. Ripples of ecstasy flooded through her, changing her, making her indelibly his.

Distantly, Alex heard her cries, and they touched him as nothing ever had. He felt the first rush and jerked. His blood roared through his veins like wildfire, burning and stinging. He buried his face in her shoulder and muffled his shout. Then, surrendering to the longest, hottest release of his life, he joined Katherine in a world where he'd never been.

It took a while for him to find himself again. Moments passed; Alex finally caught his breath and looked at her, shaking his head.

Katherine saw the look of wonder on his face and understood. She felt as if she'd just been through a hurricane. The experience was unlike anything she'd ever experienced. She couldn't possibly explain it.

"Why do I feel like I've wanted you forever?" he asked in a low voice.

She swallowed over the lump in her throat. "I don't know." Foolhardy or not, she made a decision, knowing in the end she'd miss him when he left. The idea, however, of missing Alex without having known him was far more painful. "We've got thirteen days. Let's not waste them."

Katherine was determined to make it memorable. That way, she thought, maybe he would remember her too. Tonight the stars shone in the sky, the flames burned orange, and the crowd around the campfire was halfway through the chorus of "Ninety-nine bottles of beer on the wall . . ."

She shook her head in amazement at Alex, who was eating his third hot dog. "I can't believe how much you like hot dogs. I would have thought you'd prefer caviar."

He shrugged. "Too much of a good thing. I only had a hot dog one other time. I think it was ten years ago."

"Tell your chef to fix them for dinner sometime."

Alex grinned. "He'd sooner die."

"That's understandable, considering what's in them."

He took another bite, then looked at the wiener. "What's in them?"

"Same thing that's in bologna."

"And what's in bologna?"

"It would spoil your appetite. Ask Chad tomorrow when it's not mealtime. Marshmallows are next." She opened a plastic bag and pulled out a puffy white one.

Al gave his food one more suspicious glance and tossed it into the nearest trash can. "What's in marshmallows?"

Katherine smiled. "Pure sugar."

He sat closer to her and wrapped his arm around her waist. "Like Katherine. Pure sweetness."

She skewered a few marshmallows with a coat hanger, held them over the fire, and slit her eyes at him. "I seem to recall you didn't think I was all sweetness when you first arrived."

"You're like that marshmallow," he murmured, nuzzling her hair.

"What? Burned?"

He chuckled, and the sound tickled her ear. "No. Crusty on the outside, soft and creamy on the inside."

Katherine whipped her head around, staring at him. "Does everything have a sexual connotation with you?" she whispered.

"Not everything, I don't have a single solitary sexual thought about anyone else tonight." He tugged her hair. "Lighten up, Katherine. I was talking about your personality, not your sexuality." His eyes darkened, and he leaned closer, looking pointedly at her mouth. "If you want to talk about your sexuality, though—"

Her heart hammered against her rib cage. She covered his mouth with her hand. "You're crazy."

He shot her a devilish look, then licked her finger.

Katherine gasped, jerking her hand away. "We're not alone. What in the world has gotten into you?"

He hesitated only a second, then answered seriously, "I'm having fun."

A warm and crazy kind of happiness spread through her. Her smile was slow, starting from somewhere deep inside. It seemed to match what she saw on his face. "Good." From the corner of her eye she saw the flicker of tiny little lights, and an idea struck her. "Wait here," she said, standing.

He grabbed her ankle. "Where are you going?"

Katherine's smile grew. "Just wait a minute, and I promise to give you a new and unique experience."

Reluctantly he released her. "Can I watch?"

"No."

He made a sound of exasperation. "Then what do I do?"

She shrugged. "Sing."

Alex snorted, watching her walk away. He tried to cheat, but she ducked behind some trees. He wondered what she was cooking up now. Three nights ago, everything had changed between them. Katherine wasn't fighting him anymore. Her surrender had left him feeling exhilarated, yet humbled. And if he were honest with himself, he'd have to confess that humility was a rare emotion for him.

She made him feel many things, he thought, many things he didn't understand. He stared into the fire for a few moments while the crowd swung into another song. He picked up a twig and snapped it, restless now that she was out of sight. Then he stood, looking around for her.

"You're supposed to be singing," she said from behind him.

He turned around. "You know I'm not accustomed to taking orders."

"Think of it as a new and unique experience," she teased impertinently.

His lips twitched. "You'd be in constant trouble for breaching protocol if we were in Moreno."

"Good thing I don't live in Moreno."

The faintest chill passed over him. He couldn't wholeheartedly agree with her statement. It wasn't something he wanted to examine too closely. Some things couldn't be changed. And Alex was no fool. He'd take all Katherine's magic and save it up to remember during his next terminally boring advisory council meeting.

He watched her standing there in her torn jeans and T-shirt, her hair a mass of curly copper and her eyes shining like the stars. His chest tightened. He'd never seen a more pleasing sight. He cleared his throat, nodding toward her hands. They were cupped together. "What have you got?"

"It's a gift. Hold out your hands."

"Another new and unique experience."

"Something like that," she said softly. "C'mon, open your hands."

Alex extended his palms.

She gave him an insect. "Katherine," he began, thinking it was some kind of joke. Then, when the little thing lit up, he stopped.

"It's a firefly, a lightning bug. Oops!" She cupped his hands together. "He almost got away. Do you have these in Moreno?"

He shook his head. "What do I do with it?"

"Well, if you were five, you'd catch them and put them in a jar," she instructed. "If you were a ten-year-old boy," she said in a disgusted voice, "you'd tear their lights off and put them on the sidewalk. And if you were a teenager, you'd catch them when nobody was looking. It's not cool to be fascinated with lightning bugs after you reach a certain age," she explained.

Alex peeked through his fingers, seeing a flash of green light. "And what," he asked in his driest tone, "does a thirty-three-year-old man do with a lightning bug?"

She shrugged. "You hold it for a while and look at it." Her face turned wistful, and he sensed she was talking about more than fireflies. She looked up to meet his gaze.

"Then you let it go."

For the most part reality was suspended during the following days and nights. It was as if Alex and Katherine were locked in a time capsule where it was forever summer.

Every once in a while when Katherine was alone, she gave herself a tough talk. She needed it. Having Alex's undivided passion and attention focused on her made it nearly impossible for her to keep her feet on the ground. The day he left, the bubble would burst, and she'd have to go on. She'd have to smile and be happy. She'd have to move on with her life and remember this time fondly with no regrets.

It would be extremely bad form to dress herself in black robes and check into a convent, she told herself, even if she wanted to. She started doing her nails again four days before he was scheduled to leave. The countdown had begun.

On Friday night she decided to fix a meal. Alex wanted to help. He'd somehow managed to get rid of Chad for the night.

Katherine filled a pot with water and set it on the stove. "You never told me how you got rid of Chad."

He flipped through the recipe book. "Gentlemen's agreement."

She arched an eyebrow. "Are we talking about my brother?"

"Chad's going to surprise you someday. You still see him as the little brother who's always getting into trouble, but he's growing up."

"You just liked his raunchy cigars."

He looked down his nose at her in his most royal, forbidding manner. "Shall we commence with the lasagna recipe? I'll give you the instructions, and you can—"

"Do the work." Katherine nodded and grinned. "Now why doesn't this surprise me?"

"Crush ten ripe tomatoes and —".

"Done." Katherine slapped a can of crushed tomatoes on the counter. She opened it and mixed it with the ground beef, onions, and spices simmering on the stove.

"This says you're supposed to use sausage."

"We're substituting." She dumped the lasagna noodles into the boiling water.

"The book says to watch the noodles carefully, so they'll be *al dente*."

She nodded. "Have you spent much time in the kitchen?"

"No. But I think I'll catch on quickly. First coffee, now lasagna."

Katherine didn't point out that his coffee was poured into the commode every morning. If the man wanted a fantasy, he was entitled. She rinsed the greens for the salad while he read a few more of the instructions. Then she buttered the French bread and wrapped it in foil.

"Use one pound of ricotta cheese," he continued, and frowned at the carton she put on the counter. "That's not ricotta."

Just a hint of impatience edged in. "Cottage cheese. American version. It's lower in fat and cheaper." She poured the pasta into a colander.

"Is it *al dente*?"

"Alex," she said, torn between amusement and irritation, "has anyone every told you, you can be a royal pain?"

"Is this your gentle way of suggesting that I'm not being helpful?"

She walked over to him, pulled the book from his hands, and gave him a hot, intimate kiss. She pulled back, breathing hard. His gaze was warm and inviting. She shook her head when he reached for her. "The salad dressing's in the refrigerator."

Then, as she rinsed the pasta, he said, "There's a recipe for salad dressing in this book."

She burst out laughing and turned around and shot him with the spray nozzle.

He shouted in indignation. He looked down at his drenched shirt in amazement, then at her. With murder in his eyes, he stalked over to her and grabbed the nozzle from her hands. "Do you know," he asked in a deadly threatening voice, "what we do to women who dare to spray the prince with kitchen spray nozzles?"

She struggled against the giggle in her throat and coughed. "No," she said, coughing again. "What do you do?"

Alex smiled an evil smile and shot her full force with the water. "We spray them back." Then he went one better and shot her again.

An hour later, after the lasagna had baked and they had both dried off, they sat down to enjoy the meal. "Tell me about Moreno," Katherine said as she munched on a crust of French bread.

"Our waters are the clearest turquoise. The temperature stays between sixty and ninety. The island has an Old World charm. We don't have much crime. Neighbors look out for each other. There's a lot of pride in one's work." He looked thoughtful for a moment. "I think you'd like it there. Our educational system could use some work, but the advisory council has some older members who are slow to change."

"They don't want to spend money."

"Something like that." Alex frowned, putting his fork on his plate. "There's one man in particular. Menard. I can't tell if his grudge is against me or if he's naturally contrary."

"Is he older?"

Alex nodded.

"He may be threatened by your youth. Does he have any children or grandchildren?"

Alex shrugged. "I think so. I'm usually too busy arguing with him to find out."

"I don't suppose you could fire him."

He gave a wry grin. "No. He was appointed by my father."

Katherine made a clucking sound of sympathy. "Never realized what a thankless job being a prince was."

He reached out and took her hand. "Come here and stop torturing me. You've been away too long."

Her heart melted, and she slipped from her chair and onto his lap. "The next time you see Mr. Menard, ask how many grandchildren he has. Then compliment him on his family. Maybe that'll quiet his grumblies."

"And who will take care of *my* grumblies?"

Katherine's chest tightened. She winced and tried to turn it into a smile. She touched his hair with unsteady hands. He would be leaving soon. It hurt, worse than she'd planned. She took a deep breath. "Maybe you'll find a princess or a duchess with a sense of humor."

His face grew shadowed. "But will she bring me fireflies?"

Katherine couldn't answer. The lump in her throat was too big. Her eyes began to burn.

He looked at her and swore in frustration. He pressed his mouth against hers to blot out the sadness. He held her so tightly, she felt the beat of his heart. "What are your plans for tonight, *mon ami?*" he asked in a low voice next to her ear.

Katherine closed her eyes and sighed. "I was going to take a shower, and then I thought we'd stay in if that's okay with you."

"Good," he said, and his voice held relief.

A little later, after she'd cleared away the dishes and taken a shower, Katherine unwrapped the towel from her head and began combing out the tangles from her wet hair. She started humming and stopped herself. It had been a long time since she'd even looked at it, she thought, eyeing her closet.

Too long, she decided, opening the closet door. She rummaged past the shoes and boxes until she found the box she was looking for. Sitting on the floor, she carefully lifted the porcelain music box and set it on the carpet.

It was still beautiful. The man still had his arms

clasped around the pretty lady. His head tilted toward hers; her gaze was lifted toward his.

Katherine noticed a few things she hadn't before. He held her so tightly that her dress wrinkled where he touched her. It was almost as if he were nudging her closer. And her hand didn't rest artfully on his shoulder. It clasped firmly. She seemed to be leaning into him. The man's eyes and hair were dark like Alex's. Catching herself, Katherine shook her head at her craziness.

She blew the worst of the dust off the figures and wound it up. Nothing happened. Disappointment sifted through her. It had been broken for years, she reminded herself. There was no reason it should work now. She tinkered with it for a few minutes, trying to prod it into playing.

A light knock sounded at her door, and Alex walked in. The water from his recent shower dotted his chest and kept his hair smooth. The earring, which was a secret turn-on for Katherine, winked impudently. He wore a pair of jeans that outlined his lower body with heart-stopping intimacy. His gaze for her was equally intimate. Then he caught sight of the music box. "So, there it is." He knelt beside her. "Will it play?"

"No," she said sadly. "Still broken. Beautiful, but broken. It's probably because I played it so much that summer when I was ten."

"And you think he looks like me?"

"Yes. Dark hair and eyes. Very gallant. Very intense."

He touched the lady's hair, then Katherine's. "She should have been a redhead with eyes that shine like diamonds."

"Think so?" she whispered.

Alex leaned closer and kissed her cheek. "I know so." He shoved the closet door closed and gestured toward the full-length mirror. "Look." He picked up the wide-tooth comb and pulled it through her hair. "What do you see?"

Katherine saw eyes that said too much and lips that wanted and needed. She saw a woman passionately, desperately in love. She closed her eyes against it. "I see the perm from hell."

He gave her hair a sharp tug. "Wrong. You see the kind of hair men dream about. They fantasize about burying their fingers in it."

"Honest?" Her eyes met his in the mirror. "Is that what you do?"

"Yes." He pushed the collar of her robe down to her shoulder and kissed the skin there. "I think about how your hair would feel brushing against my chest and belly. The idea"—he paused, and his lips slanted sensually—"teases me."

The idea teased her, too, but she'd wanted things to proceed differently tonight. She pulled away, standing. "You're messing up my plans. I wanted tonight to be special."

He nodded, giving her a knowing look. "That's why you insisted on separate showers."

"Yes. So I could get"—she felt flustered—"get pretty for you. Or at least try," she muttered, looking away in embarrassment.

"You already are pretty—no, beautiful." He rose to stand beside her. "But I'm curious. What would you have done?"

"I would have tried to tame my hair."

"Too late. I like it wild, anyway. What else would you have done?"

She felt silly and self-conscious. She shrugged. "Just a few things. Women things," she said, hoping that would be enough.

His gaze caressed her. "Perfume?"

She nodded.

"Makeup?"

"Just a little."

His grin was slow and very male. "Sexy lingerie?"

He was enjoying her discomfort entirely too much. Katherine tilted her nose into the air. "Possibly."

"Don't get snooty." He took her hand and looked at it. "You don't need a manicure." He frowned. "Come to think of it, you never need a manicure."

"I do them when I'm nervous. Have since I was a teenager."

He was silent for a long moment. "Your nails have been a different color nearly every day since I've been here."

"I've been nervous nearly every day since you've been here," she retorted, grabbing back her hand.

He chuckled and hugged her from behind. "So I've ruined your plans. Let me make it up to you."

Her mind filled with unbidden sensual images. She shook her head. "No, it's not—"

He quieted her by covering her mouth with his hand. It was warm and gentle. "You're still resisting me." He turned her to face the mirror. "Just for tonight, don't."

Their gazes met and mingled in the dark reflection. She felt the call of him in her blood. Her chest tightened with anticipation, while a thread of apprehension wove its way around her belly. There was a dark desire that seemed to shimmer from him, and his eyes were fathoms deep with emotion.

She didn't want to miss it, she thought. Whatever he had to give, whatever she could give him, she wanted to give, for the time they had left. She swallowed hard. "Okay."

He untied the belt of her robe. The lapels parted, revealing her bare skin, her cleavage, belly button, and the wispy auburn hair at the top of her thighs. She took a deep breath, expecting him to push the robe off her shoulders.

He did. She waited, feeling sensual in her nudity, expecting him to carry her to bed.

"Stay here," he murmured, and went to her vanity. He picked up one bottle and smelled it, then discarded it and picked up another. After the third one he nodded to himself and walked back with it in his hand.

"Would you have put it here?" he asked, rubbing the scent on her neck. He tilted the crystal bottle into his hand and slid his fingers between her breasts. "And here?"

Her throat thickened, and Katherine watched as her nipples tightened before his gaze and hers. She nodded. He smoothed his fingers down her belly, skimming to the inside of her thighs. "And here," he whispered, caressing her.

An insidious weakness threatened her knees. Her legs felt boneless, and her skin felt much too hot. She closed her eyes.

"Don't close your eyes, Katherine. I want you to see you the way I see you." He pushed her hair so that it fell over one shoulder, covering one breast. He ran his scented thumb over her shoulders and down her spine to her buttocks. Then he lost interest in the perfume, and after capping it, he carelessly shoved it back on the vanity.

"Which drawer is your gown in?"

"I can get it." She started toward him.

"No. Wait there. I'll get it. Which drawer?"

She pointed to it, and he pulled out the gown she'd chosen, a slippery piece of coral satin with lace insets on the breasts and slits on each leg.

He pulled it over her head and smoothed it down her legs to where it flirted with her thighs. The perfume was sultry, wrapping around her and him, every time they moved. Every time they breathed, it seemed. She wanted the nightgown off. She wanted his skin against her instead.

"Alex," she began.

"Lipstick and eyeliner," he said in a husky voice. "Your cheeks are already flushed."

Before she knew it, she felt the gentle glide of kohl eyeliner applied to her eyelids. His hands were warm against her hot skin. She stood still for his ministration, transfixed by his touch, by his deliberateness.

He slid coral lipstick over her lips, twice. Then, as with the perfume, he capped it and tossed it on the vanity. This time a hint of impatience bled through his movements.

Alex looked at her, his nostrils flaring. He pulled her against him. His chest was firm at her back, his arousal, full at the back of her waist. He sifted his hands through her hair, then slid his palms over breasts and belly down to her thighs. He nuzzled his face into her hair, groaning. His hands left a trail of fire that licked at her veins, making her breath come in fits and starts.

"What do you see?" he asked in a rough voice, his hands continuing to move urgently beneath the coral satin.

Her thighs trembled. "I don't know," she said helplessly. The feelings were too much, the arousal too consuming.

He made a sound of frustration and moved his hands to her breasts. "Then what do you feel, *chérie*?"

"I . . . feel . . . hot."

He laughed, and the sound was rich with passion. "So am I. What else?"

She sighed, brokenly. "Sexy," she admitted. She could hardly believe she was that woman in the mirror, the one with the full lips and come-hither eyes.

"That's right," he encouraged her, rubbing his open mouth against her throat.

Katherine arched against his moist lips. "Ohhhh. You make me feel beautiful, Alex." She lifted her hands to run her fingers through his hair.

The position was awkward, thrusting out her breasts, but she needed to touch him.

Fascinated, Alex plucked her nipples through the satin.

A moan bubbled up from her throat and escaped her lips. His eyes met hers, and something inside him seemed to snap. He nudged her head into the crook of her shoulder and made love to her mouth.

His tongue penetrated her moistness; his mouth sucked her tongue into his. He kissed her until she was achy, breathless, and clinging to him.

She wanted to face him so she could feel him against her, but he wouldn't allow it.

Katherine made a murmur of wanton dissatisfaction.

"What do you want?" he asked, his breath harsh against her hair.

"You. Dammit. You know what I want."

"Tell me." He darted his tongue into her ear.

She went dizzy from the sensation. She was so frustrated, she could cry. "I want you to get rid of those jeans," she hissed.

"Why don't you do it for me?" he taunted her.

She jerked, and there was a sensation within her of something private being torn away. Her inhibitions were burned up by the fire of his eyes.

Putting her thumbs through the loops of his jeans, she pulled him around to face her. Then, biting her lip in concentration, she released the button and slid the zipper all the way down.

She pushed his jeans down his hips and cupped him with her hands.

He swore. "Katherine—"

She shook her head. "No. You started this." She wrapped her hand around his full, throbbing erection and started stroking.

He grabbed her hands and stopped her, his chest heaving.

But Katherine felt desperate. She put her mouth against that heaving chest and licked his nipple.

"Oh, for Christ's sake," he muttered. A shudder ran through him, and he forced her away, whipping the coral satin over her head. She was on him immediately, and he stumbled out of his jeans.

Her warm mouth was on his chest again, with her hands sweet and teasing over his aching shaft. She pulled his head down and scorched him with an explicit come-and-get-me kiss.

His blood gushed through his veins like a raging flood, only hotter and much more potent. "Katherine," he muttered, striving for a shred of sanity, trying to slow down.

"No," she said against his mouth. "You wanted me this way, no holds barred. Now, you've got me. Take a look in the mirror, Alex."

She fell to her knees, and his mouth went dry. He licked his lips, vainly.

Her warm breath caressed him, making his legs shake. She rubbed her soft palms down the sides of his belly to the inside of his thighs. The sight of her painted nails so close to him made him feel like exploding. She inched closer, and he held his breath.

It was such a long, unbearable moment that he closed his eyes.

Katherine squeezed his thighs. "Open your eyes,

Alex. I want you to watch. I don't want you to forget."

He opened his mouth to assure her that forgetting was impossible, but then she touched him with her lips.

A drop of his essence slipped out, and she licked it with her tongue. His heart went wild. He watched her warm, avid mouth on him and tried to choke out a curse, but his voice wasn't working. She alternately cupped and stroked and licked him until he cried out and roughly pulled her up his body.

Her perfume swam around his head, his earlier titillation coming back to haunt him. "I'm in love with you."

Katherine went completely still and silent. Stunned, she shook her head.

"Yes, I am. And you're in love with me."

She shook her head again, her expression almost horrified.

He ran his hand down to where she was moist and soft, and stroked her. He covered her astonished mouth with his and loved her with his tongue and lips. Then he lifted her high and slid her down until she enveloped him in her tight, wet womanhood.

"Look," he said, his voice strained. "What do you see?"

Katherine looked in the mirror and saw her thighs wrapped around his waist, her breasts crushed to his chest, her eyes shiny with unshed tears.

"I see two people in love," he murmured, answering his own question.

A chime sang through his consciousness. A grind, and a soft clicking sound. The music box played. Katherine's eyes grew round. Alex hugged her to stop the trembling, but he wasn't sure which one of them was doing the trembling.

He took her to the bed, never parting from her. While the music played, he made love to her, kissing away her tears and surprise. The scent of Katherine and the sound of her music filled him, becoming a part of him. The sweet tune embedded itself in his mind as surely as Katherine had captured his heart. Alex was lost—sweetly, completely lost.

The night passed in a haze of sweat, wrenching longing, and exquisite passion. He turned to her again and again, needing to feel her touch, to hear the break of her sigh when he entered her, to see the open, honest love on her face.

He drove her relentlessly until their bodies wouldn't cooperate anymore, and they both collapsed in weak laughter. Then he curled her against him.

Katherine stared at the music box in mute wonder. If she'd had the energy to dissect the experience, she sensed it would scare her to death. Instead, she took a deep breath and let the strength of Alex's arms lull her to sleep.

❖——————————❖

The shrill ringing of the phone woke her early the next morning. Too early, she thought, looking at the alarm clock. Five A.M.

It rang again, abrasive and intruding. She scowled. Katherine lifted Alex's arm, heavy with sleep, from her shoulder. She eased out of bed and nearly fell flat on her face. Now, she understood what people meant about doing it until you can't walk.

She stiffened her rubbery legs and grabbed her robe from the floor. Carefully, putting one foot in front of the other, she tottered to the kitchen and picked up the phone.

"Hello."

The line crackled. "Hello," a feminine, desperate-sounding voice said. "Hello. I must speak to Alexander Merrick. Oh, damn. He changed his name to Al something. Al—"

"Sanders," Katherine finished for the woman. She had a sinking feeling about this phone call. "Al Sanders."

"That's right. Tell him it's Isabella. It's very important. I must speak to him, immediately. Right now."

"Gotcha," Katherine said, and set the phone on the counter. She shoved her hands through the robe and tied the sash. She took a deep breath and walked back into the bedroom. Alex was still sleeping, his face hard but content.

Katherine took a long look. "Alex, wake up" she said, careful not to touch him. "It's your sister Isabella."

His eyes blinked open. He frowned in confusion. "Isabella."

"She's on the phone."

Alex rolled his eyes, muttering. He got out of bed, and Katherine was secretly pleased to see he was nearly as unsteady on his feet as she'd been.

She followed him to the kitchen, fighting down overwhelming fear.

His voice was terse as he talked with Isabella. His mouth hardened, and he swore long and viciously. Then he seemed to come to his senses. He apologized to Isabella, thanked her for calling, and hung up.

He ran his hands through his hair and bent over the counter as if the weight of the world were on his shoulders. When he turned to Katherine, his eyes were bleak.

Her heart sank. He didn't have to say a word. She just knew.

"I must return to Moreno," Alex began as he walked toward her.

The pain of her heart breaking was so great that Katherine didn't hear the rest of what he said. And when his arms went closed around her in quiet desperation, she hurt even more. She didn't want to touch him, but she couldn't have stopped her body from nestling against him. She breathed his scent. Her throat was tight, but she managed to get out the words. "There will never be anyone like you, Alex." Her voice fell to a whisper. "Never." Katherine squeezed her eyes shut. She didn't want to cry. God help her, she didn't want to cry.

Alex was grappling with his own stunning sense of pain. "You're such a treasure, Katherine. How can I leave you?" The prospect had him resenting his position, nearly hating it. He swore softly and kissed her sleep-tousled hair, then sifted his fingers through it, realizing he would never touch her again. The sense of loss was staggering, worse than anything he'd ever experienced.

He felt her shudder, the dampness of her tears against his chest, and it was almost too much to bear.

NINE

Within an hour he was gone.

She'd watched regret and his enormous sense of duty tear at him while he'd explained that he had to return to Moreno immediately. He'd promised to call. She'd tried to smile. And their parting kiss was bittersweet.

She felt shattered into a thousand sharp pieces. She thought she'd been prepared for his leaving. She'd thought she'd be left with a melancholy but manageable sort of sadness.

But nothing could have prepared Katherine for a bed that held the scent of their lovemaking, a body that reminded her with every movement just what she'd done last night, a music box that wouldn't work, and the press.

"I really don't have any information," she said for the fifteenth time to the young reporter sniffing for blood. He stood on her front porch as immovable as the posts supporting the roof while she tried to hold her fragile self together.

"But surely, Ms. Kendall," he continued with an ingratiating smile, "you must know something of Prince Alexander. After all, he's been in your residence for—"

Chad chose that moment to stomp up the stairs. Another man in a suit followed not far behind.

Chad looked at the reporter and frowned. "Where's Al?"

Katherine bared her teeth in what she hoped looked like a smile. "He's gone." She bit her lip at the hollowness in her voice.

"Gone?"

"You were also acquainted with Prince Alexander?" asked the reporter, sensing new prey. "What can you tell us about him? His personality?" The young man flexed his pen over his pad. "His favorite foods? Anything?"

"Well, if you're talking about Al Sanders, his coffee tastes like crap." Then Chad looked as if he'd swallowed a whole lemon. "A prince?" He looked at Katherine and laughed uncertainly. "A prince? That's rich." He laughed again. "Big Napoléon. What a bunch of bull—"

Katherine winced. "Chad, there's something I need to tell you."

He chuckled, shaking his head. "Well, it can't get any better than this."

The man in the suit reached the porch. He was tall and dark. If pressed, Katherine would say he bore a faint resemblance to Alex. Her stomach tightened.

He gave a brief bow. "Ms. Kendall, my name is Jacques Merrick. I handle Prince Alexander's press relations. May I assist you?"

She felt a surge of relief at the same time she began to feel the threat of tears. She managed a nod. "Yes, thank you very much."

Chad looked from Jacques to the reporter to Katherine and narrowed his eyes. "Hey, what is—"

Katherine cleared her throat, but her voice was still shaky. "Come inside," she said desperately. "I'll fix you some breakfast and tell you all about it." She pulled his arm.

"Ms. Kendall," Jacques said, "is there a restaurant or bar?" He moved his shoulders in a Gallic shrug. "Something?"

"The grill is in the community building, but there's a better selection of restaurants on the mainland. And the ferry will be leaving soon," she added hopefully.

"Yeah," Chad said, and snickered. "And there's always Chuck's."

Watching the calculating look in Jacques's eyes, Katherine rammed her elbow in Chad's ribs.

Jacques turned to the reporter. "I have known the prince all my life, and I would be happy to give you information for your story. As a matter of fact, I happen to have some photographs in my hotel room. Shall we go?"

The command again. Katherine wondered if all the Merricks were autocratic. She felt a swift clench of worry that she'd trusted Jacques too easily. "Mr. Merrick," she said, and moved back a few steps to afford some privacy.

He shot her an impatient look. "Yes?"

"You will," she paused and whispered, "protect Alexander's image, won't you?"

He looked offended. "Of course. It is my duty to serve the royal family, and Prince Alexander is my cousin."

She sighed, still unsure. The statement sounded a little cold. "But are you Alex's friend?"

He raised an eyebrow, then shook his head. "Prince Alexander does not have many friends. His position doesn't allow for it. But you may rest assured," he said more gently, "that I will protect his reputation with my life. I have also been instructed to deflect the media from you."

She nodded, somehow reassured and unhappy at the same time, and watched Jacques lead the young reporter down the steps.

One week later Alex called. His voice hit her with the force of a body blow. It took Katherine a full minute to find her own voice.

"Katherine," said Alex, his voice edged with concern. "Are you all right?"

Her throat tightened. She wasn't sure she'd ever be all right again. She swallowed hard. "I'm fine, and you?"

"I'm working again. Funny thing, though, thoughts of a red-haired American beauty creep in at the oddest moments."

Her heart twisted. "It will pass," she assured him.

His laugh was a harsh and unhappy sound. "If you believe that, then you're terribly naive. Tell me, do you ever think of me?"

Always. Katherine rubbed her hand against her forehead. It was difficult to keep from pouring out her heart to him. Difficult, but necessary. "It doesn't matter if I think of you, Alex. When you were here, we both knew you would leave. It was inevitable."

A long silence passed. "We never discussed the future."

"Because," she said as much for herself as him, "there is no future for us."

On the other end of the line, Alex grew uneasy. He had returned to Moreno only to find he'd left the best of himself with Katherine. He wanted her with him, with a wanting that edged toward desperate need. "Why not? Moreno has airports. Your school isn't in session. You could visit. If you're worried about privacy, I have a chalet in—"

"Stop it." She took a deep breath. "This is crazy. We live in different worlds. Barring that, I have responsibilities here. I'm still trying to find a buyer. And as for your private chalet"—Katherine shook her head—"I'm not cut out for clandestine affairs."

He was stunned and incredibly hurt. "How can you say that? Nothing between us could ever be clandestine."

Katherine fought back the feelings he was rousing inside her. His voice made her feel that she was coming apart when she'd worked so hard to pull herself together. "Oh, Alex, you're fooling yourself. Everything," she said, her voice trembling, "everything about our time together was clandestine. I didn't even know your name in the beginning. We hid our involvement from everyone."

"We hid our involvement so we could have privacy and so you would be protected once I left." He managed a deep breath. "If the secrecy bothers you, I can make arrangements for a press release, and everyone will know. I wasn't ashamed, *chérie*, just selfish. I wanted you all to myself. I still want you all to myself."

Katherine felt as if she'd just stepped off a high cliff. The intensity of his feelings frightened her. It was too close to what she felt. "I know it seems that we had something—"

"—Seems! *Had?*" His composure slipped, and something like panic ripped through Alex. "*Au con-*

traire, Katherine. Have you forgotten so quickly?" Gripping the phone with a tight fist, he fought the feeling of being lost. "Have you forgotten the way we fit together? The way we can almost read each other's minds?"

Katherine closed her eyes. This was torture. "I'm not right for you. Yes. We had a very special time together, but it can't go on. I'm no blue blood, no princess or duchess. It was hard enough when you left the first time, but I couldn't bear it if it happened again. And what happens," she asked, feeling the agony squeeze her voice into something tiny and desperate, "when I embarrass you? Or worse," she said, voicing her worst fear, "when you grow tired of me?"

He said something terse and graphic in French. "You could never embarrass me. And I wouldn't grow tired of you."

The silence lengthened, and Katherine felt the distance between them grow. His world and hers. It was more than different countries, more than a different language. It was different attitudes ingrained in both of them since birth.

"Find someone else, Alex." She flinched at her suggestion, but doggedly kept on. "Someone better suited to your background. Someone who understands your duties. Someone sophisticated and tougher than I am."

Alex couldn't believe her. Her suggestion was

like a slap in the face, so horrible it seemed unreal. "That would be difficult," he said, feeling his chest tighten. "I love you."

She almost broke down then. She'd been so miserable without him, and to hear that he loved her twisted her inside out. Hearing his voice and the possibility that she could snatch a little more time with him was the most painful thing she'd ever experienced. The burning in her eyes grew worse. She felt the wetness threaten, then seep out the corners of her closed eyes.

"It's for the best, Alex," she said, hearing the fragility in her voice. "Some things are impossible."

He fought against her rationale even though he understood it. At one point he'd thought they couldn't be together. Now, he couldn't imagine *not* having her in his life. "But it is possible. We could be together. Why can't you see?"

"Because I don't want to be with you." A wayward sob escaped, and Katherine damned her slip. "I don't want to be a part of your life," she lied desperately, and wondered if lightning would strike her dead for it. Her heart contracted in protest. There was nothing more she could say. Even if she had thought of something, the painful lump in her throat would have prevented it.

"I don't believe you." He couldn't accept it, but he wondered if he'd been wrong. The doubt made his stomach turn. He'd laid himself bare for her, and she'd turned him down. His chest actually hurt. The hurt and disillusion were fresh, gaping wounds, but he had to try one more time. Like a warrior making a desperate last effort, he had to do it. "Tell me, *mon amie*," he said roughly, "that you dream of me."

Her tears ran unchecked down her cheeks. She bit her lip hard, knowing this was the hardest thing she'd done in her life. Katherine couldn't bear his distress, but she wouldn't encourage him. "I'm sorry."

A lengthy silence followed. Full. So full of everything that had passed between them, the hopes, the laughter, the passion, until there was only a deep, soundless, eternal pain.

His voice was so quiet, she barely heard him. "Call me if you change your mind. *Au revoir*, my Katherine."

The click vibrated inside her, and she held on for a long time after the line was disconnected, cuddling the phone to her ear. With trembling hands, Katherine finally hung up the phone. Then she laid her head on the kitchen table and wept, understanding what made people wish for death.

Three days later she received a Federal Express letter offering her a position as educational consultant to Moreno.

The offer caught her off guard. She shook her

head, reluctantly admiring how Alex was trying to find a suitable way for her to live in Moreno. His persistence was disarming, but the sensible part of her assured her that if she went to Moreno, she'd just be throwing herself into a situation that was doomed from the start.

She'd thought that time would lend her strength, that the days would numb her pain. So far, she'd been wrong. Her sense of loss was shattering. Chad commented on how distracted she was. She tried to make excuses, but she could see the worry in his eyes.

Instead of growing stronger, she felt herself weakening, dying for just a glance of him, wishing for the sound of his voice. She threw out her collection of nail polish, cried at the sight of fireflies, and couldn't bear to look at marshmallows. She waited two days to refuse the offer, hoping for the peace that eluded her.

It didn't come, but she stiffened her resolve and managed to write the refusal. Sending it was just one more cut from the knife.

The only positive news was an offer for the campground. When Katherine told Jasper, the relief in his voice reassured her that she'd done the right thing. The agreement was signed, and to Katherine's amazement, the holding company had requested that Chad act as interim manager.

She knew very little about the buyer, only that he

agreed to maintain the property as a campground and had the money to expedite the sale.

One evening, just as she was about to take a walk on the beach, the doorbell rang. Expecting one of the campers, Katherine opened the door. A young woman with full dark hair and dark eyes, dressed in a designer summer suit, stood on her porch with two men behind her. The young woman was looking at her with a curious, measuring air.

"Katherine Kendall?" she said in a rich, cultured voice.

Katherine nodded, instantly recognizing the faint accent. "Isabella." She paused. "Princess Isabella with-three-other-names Merrick de Moreno."

The woman arched a dark eyebrow, and her lips slowly tilted into a smile. "Yes. I do believe I understand Alex's distraction. May I come in?"

Another order couched in a question. Katherine smiled in spite of herself and moved aside as Isabella instructed the two men to wait outside. She was getting used to this.

She offered her unexpected guest a chair and some lemonade, then cut to the chase. "You're not here for the camping, are you, Your Highness?"

Isabella pulled a cigarette out of a gold case and lit it. "No, and please call me Isabella. Titles can be wearing."

Katherine wasn't totally comfortable with this

woman who seemed to know quite a bit about her, but she nodded. "Isabella."

She took a long drag from the cigarette and exhaled. "You can relax. I just want to know why you've ruined my brother."

Katherine felt the room turn sideways. She stared wide-eyed. "Ruined!"

"Well, perhaps ruined is a bit dramatic. But it's close. Alex was restless and unsettled before he went on vacation. Since he's been back, he's miserable."

Surprise ran through her. "Has he discussed this with you?" she asked doubtfully. It was difficult for her to imagine Alex willingly discussing his feelings.

"I interrogated him one evening after dinner. He was reticent at first, but after a few White Russians, he started talking"—Isabella's eyebrows wrinkled in confusion—"and singing something about ripping out his heart and stomping that sucker flat. He said some things I didn't understand. Fireflies and water-balloon battles, something about the beach at night and how beautiful she was. When I asked who she was, he said 'Katherine.'"

Her heart clenched, and she stood. Sitting was suddenly impossible. "I gave him the firefly." Katherine shrugged. "Children catch them, and he seemed to have missed out on the fun of childhood. I guess I tried to help him find that for a little while."

"Katherine, you gave my brother more than a firefly."

Katherine felt her cheeks heat. She wasn't ashamed; she just felt what she'd shared with Alex was very private. "He didn't—" she started, and faltered. Swallowing, she continued. "He didn't discuss that, did he?"

"No."

Relief coursed through her.

"But we haven't solved anything. Alex is miserable."

Feeling helpless, Katherine lifted her hands. "I don't know what to say."

"Say you'll come to Moreno."

"No."

"Why not?" Isabella challenged. "You're responsible for his unhappiness. The least you can do is visit him."

"I have responsibilities here. School starts in two-and-a-half weeks."

"Then you may visit for two weeks."

Katherine shook her head in frustration. "You don't understand. If I go, I'll just be prolonging the agony for both of us. Nothing can ever come of this. I've been involved in one major mess with a politician, and I don't want to do it again."

Isabella gave her statement a dismissing nod. "I know all about your unfortunate experience with your ex-husband. It's a drop in the bucket compared to what our family has been through. Alex probably didn't tell you about it because he feels he's got to keep the record with the press spotless to make up for our father's indiscretion."

"He mentioned something about bad choices that affected everyone," said Katherine, remembering their conversations.

Isabella sighed, flicked her ashes into the ashtray, and told Katherine the story of her parents' seven-year estrangement. Alex's young mother had been crushed when a woman came forward claiming the prince had sired her young son. The press played up the embarrassing drama.

"Oh, no," said Katherine, remembering her own humiliation.

"Oh, yes. The truth came out that while Father hadn't been responsible for producing this child, he had in fact had a lengthy affair with the woman." Isabella paused. "After he'd married my mother."

Katherine felt a surge of sympathy for Isabella's mother. She understood the feeling of betrayal. "It must have been terrible."

"It gets worse. My mother was pregnant and terribly hurt. She left my father. She took me and tried to take Alex, but my father wouldn't allow it. After all, Alex was heir to the throne." Isabella shook her head, a shadow coming over her face. "I always thought Alex got the worst of it. He was stuck with my father, who was miserable. Michellina and I got to live in the country with my mother. She was sad, but determined to make a happy life for us."

Katherine was confused. "But your parents are together now."

"Yes. It took them seven years to make up." She rolled her eyes. "They're both incredibly stubborn. Father had to court Mother all over again. The press loved that too."

Katherine's heart twisted. "And Alex?"

Sadness flickered across Isabella's face. "You're right about Alex missing his childhood. And now he has this misguided notion that he has to live a boring, unhappy life and save us from further scandal."

Katherine felt helpless. "I don't see how I can help him."

"If you care for him, you can be his friend." Isabella's gaze flickered downward. "In his position he doesn't have many."

Katherine sensed Isabella was speaking for herself too. She felt torn. Of course she badly wanted to go to Alex and make him smile and comfort him. She wanted to be there for him. But she was terrified. Going to Moreno meant she'd be risking everything. "Look at me." Katherine opened her arms, fully aware of her khaki shorts and T-shirt. She knew what her hair looked like. "I'm not princess material."

Isabella gave her an assessing glance. "We can take care of your hair, cosmetics, and wardrobe one day and leave the following day."

The cosmetics wouldn't take care of her inadequacy. Panic sliced through her, and she thought of all the obstacles. "What about my passport? Where would I stay? What about the press?"

Isabella stubbed out her cigarette. "I can arrange for a temporary visa. You'll be my guest at the palace, and Jacques will handle the press. Is there anyone you should notify of your absence?"

Katherine brushed her hair behind her ear in agitation. "My brother, Chad. He's not going to believe this. I'm not sure I do, either." Isabella was talking as if everything were decided, while Katherine was still seesawing first one way, then another. She felt uncertain, but part of her was impatient with her uncertainty. *Take a chance. You'll always regret it if you don't.*

"Fine," said Isabella, ignoring Katherine's distress. "Pack tonight. We'll leave tomorrow morning for New York."

"New York!"

"Yes," Isabella said calmly. "I've heard of a wonderful salon there. And while New York's not Paris, the shopping should be adequate."

Katherine considered backing out.

Isabella gave her a sharp glance. "Don't even think it."

Katherine shook her head, muttering, "You're worse than he is."

Isabella stopped. "What do you mean?"

"Do you always get your way?"

"No." Isabella gave a dazzling smile. "But I try."

TEN

If Alex heard one more word about Claire Deneuve's impressive pedigree, he would thrust the sterling-silver butter knife into his ribs and put an end to his misery.

"I don't want to brag," her mother said, "but, yes, Claire can trace her ancestors all the way back to Charlemagne."

Alex turned the gleaming silver knife in his hand and thought long and hard. The knife was as dull as the dinner conversation, though, and it would take quite a bit of effort to inflict a lethal stab in one stroke. Stifling a sigh, he set the knife down. It only seemed that dinner was taking an eternity, he assured himself.

His mother must have sensed his impatience. In the slightest of movements she shook her head, showing her disapproval. Her eyes held a glint of sympathy, however, and she smiled in good humor.

Claire Deneuve was the latest offering paraded under his nose as a strong suggestion for his future wife. She had all the credentials, had been to the right schools. Her reputation was spotless, her manners impeccable, and she was easy on the eyes. Her father was a wealthy, politically influential French count.

He'd heard the list of her assets *ad nauseum*. Alex wondered if she'd ever caught a firefly.

He scowled, remembering how Katherine had rejected him. His ego was bruised, his pride damaged, and he didn't want to think about what she'd done to his heart. Her implacability struck sharp and deep, leaving him with an unwelcome feeling of vulnerability.

Restless again, he looked around the linen-covered table, noticing the two empty seats. Isabella and her escort were late. Lucky them.

Claire murmured something about the weather.

Alex was about to reply when Isabella burst in. She gave a quick little bobbing curtsy, a smile full of charm. "So sorry I'm late. Please forgive me. I know it's insufferably rude."

"Yes, it is," Alex agreed dryly, noting her lack of explanation.

"I've brought a friend," she continued in a blithe tone. She opened the door and encouraged her visitor. "Come on."

Cynically he sat back and wondered what poor, unsuspecting sap Isabella had lured into her net this time. He caught a flash of red and purple. Then Alex watched as heaven and hell walked through the door in kid-leather heels.

His heart dropped to his knees. She was dressed, not in shorts, but in a purple silk dress that flowed over her curves like water. She'd cut her hair. Sentimental sorrow warred with desire. Somehow she looked both sophisticated and innocent with her lush painted mouth and large crystal eyes. He remembered painting that mouth and kissing it, watching it burn his body. He'd looked into those eyes when they turned dark with need. He stiffened, bracing himself against her effect on him.

His gaze flicked downward, and Alex caught sight of Katherine's hands, clenched at her sides. He saw through the worldly disguise. She looked terrified. Terrified but beautiful, and entirely desirable. She wouldn't meet his eyes, and he found himself irritated at the slight.

The memory of her coolly worded rejection taunted him. Masculine pride rose to the surface. He wanted to snub her, then deport her. He wanted to catch her in his arms and comfort her.

Alex nearly despised her for the flux of emotions raging inside him. His feelings for her weren't pretty or gentle. Or controlled. That fact bothered him most. What was she doing here? Was she toying with him?

Isabella ticked off introductions at the speed of sound until she came to Alex. Then she paused. "And my brother, His Royal Highness Alexander Merrick de Moreno."

Alex stood, and everyone else followed suit. "Welcome to Moreno, Ms. Kendall. We're *delighted* with your presence."

She blushed. Isabella gave her a gentle nudge. "Curtsy," she whispered.

Katherine stared at his sister in such disbelief that Alex nearly laughed out loud. Perhaps there would be justice after all.

Isabella nodded, and Katherine gave a slow, uncertain dip. "Thank you, *Your Highness*."

He moved toward her, took her hand, and kissed it. Her hand trembled within his. The movement soothed his stung ego. Something inside him bent, just the slightest bit, and he gentled his tone. "It will be my pleasure."

"Don't count on it," she whispered, taking her hand back. She looked uneasy enough to bolt.

"Please join us. We were just getting ready for the main course," Alex's mother said in mild reproof to Isabella.

Katherine was seated between the countess and the countess's son, Pierre. Alex looked at her, toying with the idea of rearranging the seating.

"How long do you plan to visit Moreno, Ms. Kendall?" Alex asked.

"Two weeks," she said, and he felt her gaze focus on his ear. She raised an eyebrow. *Where's your earring?* her eyes asked.

"Such a short time," he said, disappointed. *You cut your hair.*

"Yes, it is." She touched her hair, looking uncertain. *You don't like it.*

"It's beautiful," he reassured her, forgetting to hold his tongue.

"I'm sure Moreno is beautiful. I look forward to seeing your country."

To hell with seeing his country, Alex thought. He wanted to lock her in his suite until his passion was spent and the burning need for her disappeared. Alex watched as Pierre, wearing a pleased, seductive grin, proceeded to move in on Katherine. At that moment His Royal Highness longed for the return of the guillotine.

"Well, you've done some stupid things, but this time you've reached your peak," Katherine muttered to herself as she sat on the cushioned bench in front of her guest-room window. A vanilla-scented breeze fluttered the curtains and cooled her face. It was dark, so she couldn't see much, just the bending of trees, the shadow of ships in the harbor, a hint of a whitecap here and there.

She heard her door open and didn't turn. Another maid, she thought, and refused to get into another argument about her ability to unpack her own clothing. She'd traded her dress, heels, and stockings for her aqua cotton nightshirt emblazoned with the words WARM ME UP. Katherine rubbed her arms. She could use some warmth. Alex had been cold and remote.

Her door clicked closed, and Katherine gave a sigh of relief. She wanted to be alone.

"You cut your hair."

Her heart jumped into her throat, and she jerked her head around. He stood two feet from her, still dressed in his formal clothes, his face inscrutable. His only concession to the late hour was the loosened tie and removal of the black jacket.

She stood and swallowed hard, wishing for the millionth time that she were taller. "Isabella's suggestion. You don't like it."

"The silk dress?"

"Isabella again." She crossed her arms over her chest. "I'm afraid it will have to be dry-cleaned. I spilled some wine on it."

Alex's eyes narrowed. "Was that when Pierre invited you to his private beach?"

Katherine clenched her jaw. "No. As a matter of

fact, it was when Claire asked if you'd enjoyed slumming in America."

He didn't reply, just watched her with that cold, forbidding expression bred through hundreds of years of his ancestors. She couldn't bear it, so she slipped around him, making a wide arc to avoid him. "You don't have to worry. I won't be telling anyone about what happened between us. I'm thinking of leaving tomorrow, so—"

"Tomorrow?" he interjected. "You said you were staying for two weeks."

"Isabella's suggestion again, and my mistake for following it." She bit her lip and glanced up at him. He'd turned to face her. "Megamistake," she muttered.

He cocked his head to one side. "But you've just gotten here. Don't you want to see Moreno?"

"I've seen enough," she said flatly.

He stepped closer, and she saw that she'd been wrong about the chill in his eyes. They were bright, all right, bright with anger. "What makes you say that?" His voice was low and very controlled.

Katherine was tired of dancing around the subject. "Well, it could have something to do with the near-permanent frown you've been wearing since I arrived."

He glowered. "What should my expression be when I see the woman who told me to find someone else after I've begged her to come to me?"

Jealousy twisted her beyond reason. "It doesn't look like you wasted any time."

"My mother arranged that dinner. At least Claire doesn't hate me for being a prince."

"I never said I hated you," she retorted.

"You might as well have."

Katherine took a deep breath. "You know, Alex. That phone call was just as hard for me as it was for you. Maybe even worse. Do you think I enjoyed saying those things? Do you think I wasn't cut to ribbons? I was trying to make it easy for—"

"Easy!" Alex swore. "To throw my love back in my face."

"It sounded more like an affair to me, and I was half-tempted to take you up on your offer, Your Royal Highness. But princes don't have a corner on the market when it comes to pride and self-preservation. I have a little of my own."

They stared at each other, locked in willful combat, the air sizzling between them. It went deeper than words, and judging from his fierce expression, Alex wasn't any happier about it than she was.

She pushed her hair behind her ear and looked away. "This is crazy. I shouldn't have come. I'm sorry for all the grief I've caused you." She walked to the dresser and pulled the music box from the drawer. "But I do want you to have this." She pushed it into his hands.

He looked dumbfounded. "Why?"

"Open it."

He looked at her, then down at the box, and opened it. The tiny grind of gears broke the silence, and the music played. He listened for a moment, his face gentling with memories. Katherine felt the tug of them too. Her skin grew warm and her breath short at the vivid images playing in her mind.

Abruptly Alex closed the lid with a click and reached past her to set it on the dresser. "I don't want the damned music box. I want you."

Katherine froze. Stunned by the blunt need in his voice, she helplessly watched him move toward her with purpose stamped on his rigid features. A second later his arms went around her, warm and encompassing. Katherine closed her eyes against her immediate, unbidden response. Like a flower toward the sun, her body curled into his heat. Her hands sought the strength of his shoulders.

"I'm starving for you," he muttered roughly. "I want to drink your laughter until I'm drunk with it. I want to taste your body until you cry out. I want too much."

Her heart twisted. She bowed her head into his chest. "Two weeks," she said desperately. "I'm leaving in two weeks."

His hands tightened around her waist, and he nuzzled her hair. "If I had my way, I'd lock you in my suite."

"The press would have a field day."

"Don't push me, Katherine."

The recklessness in his voice made her uneasy. She looked up and touched his jaw. He was so precious to her that she ached. "I lied," she whispered. "I did dream of you."

His gaze darkened, and he smoothed the hair from her face. "You won't for the next fourteen days."

Confused, she rubbed her cheek against his hand. "Why?"

A hint of an arrogant grin tugged at his lips. "You won't be sleeping."

She did sleep, but only in the early hours before dawn when Alex left her. The nights were his. Katherine didn't question the way he demanded rights to her body, because, right or wrong, she felt the same way about him.

On Tuesday morning Alex cleared his schedule and took Katherine on a tour of Moreno in, of all things, a carriage.

She noticed the way everyone from shopkeepers to professionals dressed in suits waved and deferred to him. It must be a heady experience to be always the center of attention, she thought, as they rode through the market square with the quaint, colorful buildings. She wondered if it might also get lonely, though, when everyone expected you to be at your best all the time.

Pride and devotion came through in his voice as he told her the history of his country. Katherine was charmed by the mingling of French and English she heard, but mostly she was charmed by the man beside her.

When they meandered onto a quiet lane that bordered the palace, the time-zone change began to catch up with her. Katherine shook her head. "Well, I can honestly say I've never done this before."

Alex took her hand and grinned. "Done what?"

"A carriage ride at dawn with a prince."

He chuckled. "Not exactly dawn. It's ten-thirty."

"Well it feels like dawn. I've been awake the past two nights."

"Do you wish I'd let you sleep?" he asked, his gut twisting at how eager he'd been to show her Moreno. It was important to him. Somewhere inside him, he realized he was still trying to sell her on the idea of staying here. If he couldn't hold her on his own, then perhaps the charm of his country would help win her over.

Katherine muffled a yawn. "When?"

"Last night or this morning." The joy had gone out of his voice. She heard it immediately. Katherine leaned closer to him and lifted his sunglasses so she could see his eyes. Need and caution shone, and she wished she could wipe them away. She reached up and pressed her mouth to his. "I was joking. I can sleep the rest of my life. I just want to be with you."

His eyes darkened, and he kissed her so passionately that her mind turned to mush for the rest of the ride.

The next afternoon he took her to a private beach where the sand was pure white and the waters clear turquoise. He told her he'd come here often as a child. She remembered how he'd been separated from his mother and sisters. "Was it lonely?"

He looked at her and shook his head in awe. "You're very perceptive, *chérie*. I missed my family. When I walk here, in the future, I'll think of Katherine with the wind blowing her hair and the smile curving her lips." He touched her hair and lips, thoughtfully.

"I have something for you," he said, reaching into his pocket. He held out his palm to her, and inside it was a gold firefly with an amber stone for its light. "You can wear it on a chain or bracelet."

Katherine's heart caught. It meant too much to her. She felt her hands begin to shake. She wanted to make sure that he'd never be lonely again, but she couldn't. The truth tore at her. Maybe they shouldn't be building these precious memories. "You shouldn't give me presents."

"It pleases me to give you gifts."

The hint of arrogance was back in his voice, enough to keep her from making a fool of herself and crying over a jeweled gold charm. "And we certainly wouldn't want to displease His Royal Highness, would we?"

He nodded in approval and placed the trinket in her hand. Then he closed her fingers and kissed them. "That's right. We wouldn't."

Her heart lightened in spite of her. "Just out of curiosity, what kind of punishment does Prince Alexander dole out when he's been *displeased*?" She couldn't contain a naughty grin. "Are we talking about a little bondage in the dungeon, or whips and chains?"

A dangerous glint came into his eyes. "It depends on the crime and the criminal. For a red-haired witch with crystal-clear eyes," he said in a silky voice as he pulled her against him, "I show no mercy."

And Lord knows, he didn't. A few days later he gave her another charm, a crystal shell. He said it reminded him of her eyes and their time together at Pirate Island. That week was glorious, but something changed at the beginning of her last seven days in Moreno, and she felt him begin to retreat.

He still came to her every night with the same desperate need and unbridled passion. What bothered her, though, was what happened when they weren't in bed.

Alex was distant. With each passing day Katherine began to realize the enormous burden of his position. When she broached the subject with him, he brushed it aside, saying he didn't want to waste what little time they had talking about him. She cared too much not to be frustrated by his remote attitude, especially since she knew how open he could be.

One afternoon she was on her way out of the palace, intending to go for a walk on the beach, when Alex's mother spotted her and had a servant request her presence for tea.

Katherine tried not to grimace. "Of course," she said, entering the drawing room. She swallowed, then curtsied, noticing Alex's father, Prince Philippe, was also present.

Princess Noelle Merrick was an exquisitely beautiful woman with dark hair and lively dark eyes. "Ms. Kendall, I understand Alex met you during his recent vacation in America."

Katherine gave a tight smile and accepted a cup of tea. The china was the finest and most delicate she'd ever held. She hoped she didn't crush it between her fingers. "Yes, he did."

Noelle furrowed her delicate brow. "I never quite understood how he happened to get on that island. What was the name of it?"

"Pirate Island. It was a rainy night. There was a detour, and Alex had to check his directions." Katherine wouldn't dream of telling them the whole story of how his security had lost track of him. "Then he met my brother," she muttered.

"Alex is so industrious, we almost have to trick

him into taking a vacation. I'm curious. He was on your island for four weeks. What did he do?"

"Noelle," Prince Philippe intervened.

Katherine looked at both of them and realized they, too, felt distant from their eldest son. Noelle's question wasn't asked out of intrusiveness. It was asked with a hopeful kind of motherly desperation to know the son she'd been forced to leave behind so long ago.

Katherine made an instant decision, knowing it was a gamble, hoping that in the long run it would make Alex's life happier. "It's okay," Katherine said. "Alex didn't tell us he was a prince until near the end of his visit."

Prince Philippe looked appalled.

Katherine rushed to explain. "I think he wanted, just once, to be thought of as an average man. I'm sure you can understand that."

Prince Philippe hesitated, then nodded.

"So he worked at the campground. He fought in a water-balloon battle. He taught some children how to shadow-fence with switches. He helped win a greased-flagpole race. He was a pirate in a skit performed for the guests. And he ate hot dogs." *And made me fall in love with him*.

Two teacups poised in midair as Philippe and Noelle looked at Katherine uncomprehendingly.

"Water-balloon battle?" Philippe said.

"Greased flagpole?" Noelle said.

Katherine explained the dynamics of a water-balloon battle, and the strategy involved in a greased flagpole race. Alex's parents laughed, devouring every story. She gave them a new picture of their son, but she left out the ear-piercing incident. And she didn't begin to try to explain her relationship with Alex. How could she?

Philippe shook his head. "And no one ever suspected he was royalty?"

"No," she said feeling suddenly protective. "You know how responsible Alex is. He would never do anything that would reflect poorly on your family. His first duty is to his country. He could never forget that." She bit her lip, searching their faces. "I hope I haven't made you lose respect for Alex by telling you all this. He's a wonderful leader, and he cares so deeply about Moreno and your family. Sometimes he seems remote, but it's not because he doesn't care."

"It sounds as if you know my son very well," said the prince, lighting a cigarette.

Katherine felt her cheeks heat. "I just saw him in a different environment."

Noelle looked thoughtful. "How much longer will you be staying with us?"

Katherine felt her happiness take a nosedive. "I'll be leaving in three days."

"So soon," Noelle exclaimed. "We'll be sad to see you go. Perhaps you can come again."

"Perhaps," Katherine replied. *Perhaps not.*

⸺◈⸺⸺⸺⸺⸺◈⸺

The following evening Katherine was nearly as tense as Alex was. Her imminent departure weighed on her heart like a three-hundred-pound ball and chain. She didn't feel right about going, but she couldn't possibly stay. In an odd way she felt fiercely protective of Alex, of his heart and his tenderness. Anyone else would call it laughable. Anyone else would point out there'd never been a more self-sufficient man on the earth.

And, of course, in a way, she'd have to agree. Looking at him now as he greeted the members of the security council and their wives, she thought he looked as cool as the steel blade of his sword. She watched from afar, remaining firmly in the background at tonight's cocktail party. The purpose of the party was clear: to strengthen alliances and pour oil on potentially troubled waters.

It would probably work a heck of a lot better if he'd smile every once in a while.

"Are you dying of fun yet?" a feminine voice said beside her.

Katherine looked at Isabella and shook her head. "Not yet. It's interesting seeing the different dynamics of this group."

"Is that a polite way of saying these refined gentlemen are actually a group of vultures ready to go for the jugular at the first opportunity?"

Katherine gave a half-smile. "I wouldn't have phrased it exactly that way."

Isabella shrugged. "They'd pick Alex clean if they could. You can't claw ice, though."

Katherine looked at Alex again and frowned. "Is he always like this?"

Isabella nodded. "The more upset, the cooler he gets."

At that moment Alex had a break in greeting people. He flicked his gaze over to Katherine. He didn't say a word, didn't crook his finger, didn't raise an eyebrow, but she heard the command loud and clear. *Come here*.

She cocked her head to one side and paused.

He must have caught the message. His eyes glinted, and his lips lifted slightly. *Please*.

Katherine waltzed over, her smile growing with every step closer. "Hi, how's it going?"

His face was calm, but his gaze was turbulent. "Fine," he said. "Everything's under control." He took her hand and clasped it within the folds of her skirt.

"It looks like everything's a little too controlled to me," she murmured, feeling her heart jump at the touch of his hand.

Alex looked at her sharply. "You've seen me out of control on more than one occasion during the last eleven days," he said in a low, precise voice.

"In bed, not out," she returned bluntly.

He raised an eyebrow. "You know I'm not choosy about the place as long as it's you. If you'd like more variety, I can—"

"Stuff it, Alex." Exasperated, Katherine tore her hand from his. "I'm leaving."

"No," he said a little louder than he'd intended. He pushed down the panic crowding his throat. "Stay a little longer. Please," he added when she shook her head.

"There's a gray-haired man and his wife headed this way. My place is in the corner. Besides, if I stay, I'll be tempted to pinch you or jab you with a pin just to see if you're real."

She flounced away, and Alex balled his fists to check the impulse to jerk her back into his arms. He watched her go, and a wave of helplessness nearly swept him away with its force. She would be leaving in thirty-five hours.

He'd promised himself he would take what she offered and not ask for more, but he spent his moments thinking of ways to prolong her stay. He could close the airport for the day. He could halt departures from the harbor. He could arrange for her papers to be misplaced, permanently.

He swore under his breath. Katherine would appreciate the heavy-handed arrogance in all those actions, he thought cynically. What she didn't understand was that he was a desperate man.

His body tensed as his least-favorite security-council officer stepped forward. "Good evening, Mr. Menard," Alex said, "are you enjoying yourself?"

The older man gave a little bow. "Yes, thank you, Your Highness. It appears we'll have a split when it come to the new health plan."

Always the bearer of good news, Alex thought. "Things can change by the time for the vote," he said in a cool voice. "It's early yet."

Menard shook his head. "It doesn't look hopeful to me."

At that moment Alex's mother walked up and kissed him on the cheek. Surprised, he stiffened. His mother wasn't often publicly demonstrative with him.

"Your father and I enjoyed tea with Katherine yesterday. She's a delight." Princess Noelle gave a wide smile. "My favorite story was the water-balloon battle. I nearly laughed until I cried."

Speechless, he stared at her. Fortunately she took over the conversation with Menard. Alex narrowed his eyes, looking for Katherine, but in the crush of the crowd, he couldn't spot her. What, he wondered, had possessed her to tell his parents about his time at Pirate Island?

He recovered from the shock and gathered his composure around him like armor. He was well practiced at it. This week he'd done it every morning after he'd left Katherine amid love-scented sheets where he'd lost himself inside her time and time again. He'd kept the days rigidly divided from the nights, knowing he was riding the edge of sanity by being with her and knowing she would leave.

A few minutes later his father strode to his side and murmured something about adding a greased-flagpole race to International Games Week. Then Prince Philippe chuckled and nudged Alex with his elbow.

Alex ordered a drink.

Isabella came up and murmured, "You need to loosen up, Alex. You look like the maid put too much starch in your shorts."

Alex gave a long-suffering sigh. "I'm not in the mood for it tonight, Isabella. Go find someone else to torment."

"Tormenting you is the only way I get an honest response."

That turned his head. He wondered if his entire family felt that way. At a loss, he pushed a hand through his hair. "Then why did you bring Katherine to me?"

Isabella's face softened. "She's a gift. I knew it the first time I met her."

"You never told me how you got her to come."

She shook her head. "It's a secret. Speaking of secrets, though . . ." She smiled mischievously, pushing back her hair to display her elaborate diamond-and-pearl earring. "Want to borrow it? I imagine you don't have much of a selection to choose from."

Isabella knew. He wondered what else she knew. Alex felt a ripping sensation inside him. He was ready to yell, throw his glass of whiskey against the wall, and start a bloody brawl. "*Where is she?*"

Isabella backed away at the tone of his voice. "Who?"

"Katherine," he bit out, searching the crowd.

"I don't know," Isabella said. "I haven't seen her in a while. I was just teasing a little bit, Alex. No need to get upset." His sister was racing her sentences, something she only did when she was worried. "Let me get you another drink. Have you had anything to eat? What about—"

"Never mind." Alex spied the redhead in a distant corner. She was sneaking her foot from one of her black high heels. He started walking. "I'll get her."

It took him less than two minutes to get to the other side of the room. He clasped Katherine's wrist. "Let's go."

Katherine's head shot up, and she looked at him in wide-eyed confusion. "Go? I thought you had to give a speech."

"I do," he said, calmly pressing his palm into her back and pushing her forward.

Katherine crammed her foot back into the shoe

and stumbled along. "Where are we going? When are you supposed to speak?"

Alex dragged her down the marble-floored hall past a group of people who stared after them. "To my suite." He glanced at his Rolex. "I'm scheduled to speak in three minutes."

She hopped up the stairs trying to keep up with him. "Three minutes! Shouldn't you be down there now?"

"They'll wait. I'm the prince." He pulled her into the room and slammed the door shut and turned the lock. "Remember?" He nudged her past the sitting area into another room, and slammed that door behind her too.

Katherine heard the click of the lock and felt a shiver of premonition. She'd never been in his bedroom before.

He flicked on the light and stepped toward her. Seeing the flinty look in his eyes, she automatically took a step back.

"My mother says she loved the water-balloon story. My father wants to do a greased-flagpole race for International Games Week. And," he said in amazed fury, "Isabella offered to lend me her earring. What else have you told my family?"

Katherine stiffened, lifting her chin. She was darn tired of his cold complacency. "I did it for your own good. Those people care for you, but they can't get past your royal force field. It was the least I could do for them, if not for you."

"Who gave you permission—"

"I don't have to ask permission! I love you!" Realizing she was shouting, she lowered her voice and wandered past the huge bed. "If I'm not going to be here, the least I can do is make sure your family sees past your iron composure for the man you are. I want them to know how caring you are." She turned to glare at him. "Not that you're helping my case one bit."

He stalked over to her. "Did you ever think I'm hanging on to this damned composure by a hangnail? Did you ever once think that I'm not particularly happy that you're leaving?"

"No, I didn't. I've been too busy wondering whether I'll meet Jekyll or Hyde the next time I see you. You know," she continued even though the light in his eyes had turned dangerous, "if you'd show the slightest bit of humanity, I might be tempted to stay. But you're too busy competing with an igloo—"

"Not in bed," he cut in.

Katherine rolled her eyes and looked down at the mammoth bed. She jerked a pillow from beneath the covers and shook it at him. "Not in bed. Not in bed. Can't you get it through your head that there's more to this than sex?"

Frustrated beyond words, she curled her hands

into the pillow and impulsively, recklessly, whomped him with it. The delicate fabric caught on one of the medals on his chest and ripped, releasing a puff of downy feathers.

Alex looked at her as if she'd lost her mind. "What are you doing?"

The gray feathers clung lovingly to his dress white uniform. A few of them sifted down to his shoes. The sight both appalled and delighted her. "Oh, my goodness." She laughed nervously, brushing the feathers from his chest. "I guess I started a pillow fight." She laughed again, and coughed to cover the sound.

He grabbed the pillow. "And the purpose of a pillow fight is?" The slightest edge of menace crossed his face.

Katherine backed up and bumped into the edge of the bed. "I, uh, guess to hit people with pillows and have fun."

"That's all," he said, shifting his grip on the pillow. "Just hitting and having fun. I want to make sure I understand this."

She nodded mutely. The devil was in his eyes, and it looked like the master of self-control was getting ready to lose it. Her heart beat an unsteady rhythm. He could do anything to her, she thought wildly, glancing at the bed. If she screamed, no one would hear. Heaven help her, she was so excited, she could hardly bear it. She braced herself for his wild passion.

He thumped the pillow over her head. Katherine stared at him in disbelief. More feathers seeped from the tear. "Alex—"

He thumped again, this time on her bottom. She opened her mouth, but it was instantly filled with pillow before she could get out a word. She fell onto the bed, reaching in self-defense for another pillow. Alex came after her with vengeance.

"You witch," he accused. "You storm into my life, wreak havoc with my libido, steal my sanity, and—"

Katherine's fingers reached the pillow. "I didn't storm into your life. You stormed into mine."

He lifted his pillow.

She shrieked, and he gave a low, dirty laugh. She ducked and slammed him instead. The battle ensued, with Katherine scrambling to roll off the bed and Alex relentlessly bonking her with his depleting pillow.

When his pillow went flat, he stole hers. In a matter of seconds she found herself flat on her back with Alex sitting on her. "No fair!" she cried breathlessly. "I'm unarmed."

He stared down into her face, his breath heavy from chasing her and laughing. "That's what I say. No fair. You've stolen my heart and left me unarmed." He leaned down and kissed her. His mouth said it all as he searched and asked, but didn't demand.

Katherine yielded, twining her arms around his neck, sifting her fingers through his hair.

He moaned.

A feather drifted between their cheeks, tickling them apart. He held her hand against his jaw, closing his eyes.

Her heart swelled inside her chest.

He opened his eyes. "Katherine, you have to stay."

Her pulse jiggled. "Why?"

He brushed her hair from her face. "Because if you don't stay, I'll have no one to teach my children how to pillow-fight."

Her mouth went dry. "This sounds serious."

"It is. I want you here with me. I want my babies growing in your belly. And I swear if I have to, I'll chain you to my bed."

She took a deep breath. "Ever thought about just asking me?"

He hesitated for a long moment. The silence in the room was unnerving. Katherine restrained the urge to fill it with meaningless chatter. He took her hand and looked deep into her eyes, letting her see his stunning need. "Will you marry me?"

Her throat closed up. She'd dreamed those words. She'd also known she'd never hear them. She swallowed hard, rushing to warn him of all her deficiencies. "My father's no French count, and I'm no blue blood. I'm not even a citizen of Moreno. I don't know when I'm supposed to curtsy and when I'm not supposed to. I—"

He put his other hand over her mouth, and a grim smile played on his lips. "It doesn't matter. You'll become a citizen of Moreno, and it will be my pleasure to tell you when to curtsy to me."

She'd just bet it would.

"You haven't answered me."

Her voice came out muffled. "You're covering my mouth."

He instantly removed his hand. "One word," he said, "and it better be the right one."

"Yes," she said decisively, then rushed on because she would never be a totally submissive woman. "But you've got to promise to try to loosen up, at least with your family. They care about you."

Alex paused and looked away. "It's—difficult for me. When my mother and sister left, I felt abandoned and angry. When they returned, it was expected that everything should go back to the way it was. My father never discussed it. My mother tried once," he said with a grim smile that pinched Katherine's heart, "but I was a teenager and knew it all then." He looked at Katherine. "Am I making any sense?"

She nodded. "You needed someone who understood your point of view."

"Yes." His voice grew rough. "I wish I'd known you then."

Katherine's eyes welled with tears. "Oh, Alex. I wish I'd been there for you. I will be now." Katherine finally realized that even a prince could fear abandonment.

His gaze was tender. "You make it easy to open up. Knowing you'll stay makes all the difference in the world. I love you." He kissed her. "More than life."

Euphoric, she laughed through her tears. She looked at him through blurry eyes, filled with joy that he trusted her so completely. "I don't know what to say. You've made me so happy."

"You've done the same for me, *chérie*." He gazed at her intently, and she saw the power of his love for her. It was awesome. "There is," he said, and the smile that grew on his face was easy to read, "only one thing that will make me more happy right now."

"Anything. Any . . ." Her voice faded as he slowly and deliberately pushed her dress up her legs and unsnapped a garter without removing his gaze from hers. She felt a rush of heat at the touch of his hands on her thighs. She cleared her throat. "What are you doing?"

"Getting ready." He unsnapped the other garter and slipped first one stocking down her leg, then the other. His finger stretched under the edge of her panties.

She cleared her throat again. "Getting ready to do what? Alex, really, you're supposed to be giving a speech."

He tugged the panties down her legs and tossed them aside. Then he quickly rid himself of his jacket and shirt. "I'm sure the security advisers would agree that what I'm doing now is far more important than delivering a speech. Lift up, darling." He pulled the dress over her head. When he saw she wore no bra, he made an approving sound.

Katherine felt aroused, excited, and guilty as sin on Sunday with all those people downstairs waiting for him. She tried to be practical. "This can wait," she said, watching him lower his zipper and release his straining masculinity.

He shook his head, wearing the "I'm gonna eat you alive" look. "I'm ensuring the line, Katherine Kendall, soon to be Princess Katherine Merrick de Moreno." He fluttered his fingers over her taut nipples, down her ribs and abdomen, to the dampness between her legs. His thumb glanced the nub while he eased his finger inside her. He watched her all the while.

Katherine felt light-headed.

Then, suddenly, it was his hard, bare erection poised at the entrance to her femininity. His chest caressed her nipples. He rubbed his masculinity against her, teasing her, teasing himself. His breath hissed with the slick contact. "Any objections?"

She shook her head.

"Take note, Katherine," he said in a passion-strained voice. "We're not—" He thrust inside her.

He closed his eyes at the pleasure and swore. "My *chérie*, we're *not* in bed."

EPILOGUE

·

"He's besotted," Mr. Menard said. "Absolutely besotted."

The old man was behind her, but Katherine could make out his voice. She leaned a little closer.

"I think she's done wonders for him," Mrs. Menard said. "He actually smiles now."

"I can't disagree with you on that." Mr. Menard sniffed. "Was a cold fish before. Do you know he asked to see pictures of the grandchildren the other day? Said Letitia was a beauty and that little Arnold looked like he'd inherited my good strength."

Katherine heard the pride in his voice and smiled.

"Always knew the prince was sharp as a whip. Guess he just needed the right woman."

Distracting Katherine from her eavesdropping, Uncle Jasper came alongside her and caught her in an affectionate hug. "So, he finally found you," Jasper said. "The man on the music box."

Katherine's eyes widened in surprise. "How did you know?"

"Uncles know everything. Have you forgotten?"

Torn between laughing and rolling her eyes, she shook her head. "No. I haven't forgotten the important things like how to catch a fish and that honesty always works best. I also haven't forgotten how a certain man took the time to teach a little girl about love. I'm very lucky to have such a wonderful uncle. Thanks," she said, reaching up to kiss his cheek.

She watched him fight the mistiness in his eyes and felt the same clutch of emotion inside her.

He shook his head. "I'm the lucky one, Katie," he said gruffly. He cleared his throat and released her. "I think your man's headed this way. He can have this dance, but you save one for me," he muttered and melted into the crowd.

Katherine watched him go for a minute, then turned and smiled wide, spotting Alex, devastating in black formal attire, stride toward her. His diamond earring stud winked at her with sexy glee.

"Time for our waltz, darling. I selected the music myself."

Katherine nodded and took his arm. "Have you talked to Chad?"

"About anything in particular?"

"The book he's planning to write about our courtship. He says it'll make him a millionaire."

Alex gave a long-suffering groan. "Did you tell him about our dungeons?"

"No. I showed him. I also told him that he wouldn't want to get himself fired from his position as manager of Pirate Island Campground. He was surprised when I told him you were the one who'd bought it. Then I pointed out that I could make his life a living hell with my newly gained position as the princess of Moreno."

Alex's mouth twitched. "I'm so glad to see you're using your new power appropriately."

"I learned from the best."

He laughed, then ushered her to the center of the dance floor. A hush descended over the festive wedding reception, and Katherine felt a hint of nervousness at all the attention she was receiving. When she looked into Alex's eyes, though, she felt steadied.

She bent in a deep curtsy. Alex took her into his arms, and the music began. Sweet and poignant, the tune wasn't the traditional wedding waltz. It was Paganini. Her heart tightened in her chest, and a wave of memories washed over her. She felt tears threaten.

Alex squeezed her waist. "I knew you'd cry," he whispered, kissing her forehead.

She inhaled hard, trying to blink back the tears.

"You didn't know I'd give you that earring as a wedding present."

"You didn't know I'd wear it. And I knew you'd get pregnant that night in my suite."

"I'm not sure how that happened," she murmured, still amazed that his prediction had come true. She was now carrying a part of Alex inside her. It shook her every time she thought of it. "It wasn't the right time."

His face lost a bit of overwhelming confidence. "You are happy about it?"

"Incredibly. I just can't believe it." Her eyes filled with tears again. "I love you so much, and I dreamed of you, but I never dreamed I'd be so—"

Alex pressed his mouth over hers, stopping the flow of words, but not the emotion that was like a strong river flowing between them.

The kiss went on and on, past the whispers, the titters. Finally he pulled back from her when the guests broke into applause.

"You've given me life and love, *mon amie*," he said, his voice tense and husky, his eyes full of emotion. "My heart is yours."

Their gazes locked in love and joy. The moment was powerful and intimate. "And my heart is yours," she whispered, thinking she'd belonged to him even before she'd met him.

Katherine took a deep breath, knowing they both needed to gather their composure. The reception had only begun. She looked pointedly at his ear. "Your Highness, your earring is very, very distracting." She lowered her voice in invitation. "Will you wear it *all night*?"

Heat flared in his eyes. His smile was full of threats and promises, all designed to send her into a frenzy. She felt the first of it rushing through her blood.

"Darling, it will be my pleasure."

THE EDITOR'S CORNER

Let the fires of love's passion keep you warm as summer's days shorten into the frosty nights of autumn. Those falling leaves and chilly mornings are a sure signal that winter's on the way! So make a date to snuggle up under a comforter and read the six romances LOVESWEPT has in store for you. They're sure to heat up your reading hours with their witty and sensuous tales.

Fayrene Preston's scrumptious and clever story, **THE COLORS OF JOY,** LOVESWEPT #642 is a surefire heartwarmer. Seemingly unaware of his surroundings, Caleb McClintock steps off the curb—and is yanked out of the path of an oncoming car by a blue-eyed angel! Even though Joy Williams had been pretending to be her twin sister as part of a daredevil charade, he'd recognized her, known her when almost no one could tell them apart. His wickedly sensual experiments will surely show a lady who's adored variety that one man is all she'll ever need! You won't soon forget this charming story by Fayrene.

Take a trip to the tropics with Linda Wisdom's **SUDDEN IMPULSE,** LOVESWEPT #643. Ben Wyatt had imagined the creator of vivid fabric designs as a passionate wanton who wove her fiery fantasies into the cloth of dreams, but when he flew to Treasure Cove to meet her, he was shocked to encounter Kelly Andrews, a cool businesswoman who'd chosen paradise as an escape! Beguiled by the tawny-eyed designer who'd sworn off driven men wedded to their work, Ben sensed that beneath her silken surface was a fire he must taste. Captivated by her beauty, enthralled by her sensuality, Ben challenged her to seize her chance at love. Linda's steamy tale will melt away the frost of a chilly autumn day.

Theresa Gladden will get you in the Halloween mood with her spooky but oh, so sexy duo, **ANGIE AND THE GHOSTBUSTER,** LOVESWEPT #644. Drawn to an old house by an intriguing letter and a shockingly vivid dream, Dr. Gabriel Richards came in search of a tormented ghost—but instead found a sassy blonde with dreamer's eyes who awakened an old torment of his own. Angie Parker was two-parts angel to one-part vixen, a sexy, skeptical, single mom who suspected a con—but couldn't deny the chemistry between them, or disguise her burning need. Theresa puts her "supernatural" talents to their best use in this delightful tale.

The ever-creative and talented Judy Gill returns with a magnificent, touching tale that I'm sure you'll agree is a **SHEER DELIGHT,** LOVESWEPT #645. Matt Fiedler had been caught looking—and touching—the silky lingerie on display in the sweet-scented boutique, but when he discovered he'd stumbled into Dee Farris's shop, he wanted his hands all over the lady instead! Dee had never forgotten the reckless bad boy who'd awakened her to exquisite passion in college, then shattered her dreams by promising to return for her, but never keeping his word. Dee feared the doubts that had once driven him away couldn't be silenced by desire, that Matt's pride might be stronger than his need to possess her. This one will grab hold of your heartstrings and never let go!

Victoria Leigh's in brilliant form with **TAKE A CHANCE ON LOVE**, LOVESWEPT #646. Biff Fuller could almost taste her skin and smell her exotic fragrance from across the casino floor, but he sensed that the bare-shouldered woman gambling with such abandon might be the most dangerous risk he'd ever taken! Amanda Lawrence never expected to see him again, the man who'd branded her his with only a touch. But when Biff appeared without warning and vowed to fight her dragons, she had to surrender. The emotional tension in Vicki's very special story will leave you breathless!

I'm sure that you must have loved Bonnie Pega's first book with us last summer. I'm happy to say that she's outdoing herself with her second great love story, **WILD THING**, LOVESWEPT #647. Patrick Brady knew he'd had a concussion, but was the woman he saw only a hazy fantasy, or delectable flesh and blood? Robin McKenna wasn't thrilled about caring for the man, even less when she learned her handsome patient was a reporter—but she was helpless to resist his long, lean body and his wicked grin. Seduced by searing embraces and tantalized by unbearable longing, Robin wondered if she dared confess the truth. Trusting Patrick meant surrendering her sorrow, but could he show her she was brave enough to claim his love forever? Bonnie's on her way to becoming one of your LOVESWEPT favorites with **WILD THING**.

Here's to the fresh, cool days—and hot nights—of fall.

With best wishes,

[signature: Nita Taublib]

Nita Taublib
Associate Publisher

P.S. Don't miss the exciting big women's fiction reads Bantam will have on sale in September: Teresa Medeiros's **A WHISPER OF ROSES,** Rosanne Bittner's **TENDER BETRAYAL,** Lucia Grahame's **THE PAINTED LADY,** and Sara Orwig's **OREGON BROWN.** We'll be giving you a sneak peek at these terrific books in next month's LOVESWEPTS. And immediately following this page look for a preview of the spectacular women's fiction books from Bantam *available now!*

Don't miss these exciting books by your
favorite Bantam authors

On sale in August:
*THE MAGNIFICENT
ROGUE*
by Iris Johansen

VIRTUE
by Jane Feather

*BENEATH A SAPPHIRE
SEA*
by Jessica Bryan

TEMPTING EDEN
by Maureen Reynolds

And in hardcover from Doubleday
WHERE DOLPHINS GO
by Peggy Webb

Iris Johansen

nationally bestselling author of
THE TIGER PRINCE

presents

THE MAGNIFICENT ROGUE

Iris Johansen's spellbinding, sensuous romantic novels have captivated readers and won awards for a decade now, and this is her most spectacular story yet. From the glittering court of Queen Elizabeth to a barren Scottish island, here is a heartstopping tale of courageous love . . . and unspeakable evil.

The daring chieftain of a Scottish clan, Robert McDarren knows no fear, and only the threat to a kinsman's life makes him bow to Queen Elizabeth's order that he wed Kathryn Ann Kentrye. He's aware of the dangerous secret in Kate's past, a secret that could destroy a great empire, but he doesn't expect the stirring of desire when he first lays eyes on the fragile beauty. Grateful to escape the tyranny of her guardian, Kate accepts the mesmerizing stranger as her husband. But even as they discover a passion greater than either has known, enemies are weaving their poisonous web around them, and soon Robert and Kate must risk their very lives to defy the ultimate treachery.

"I won't hush. You cannot push me away again. I tell you that—"

Robert covered her lips with his hand. "I know what you're saying. You're saying I don't have to shelter you under my wing but I must coo like a peaceful dove whenever I'm around you."

"I could not imagine you cooing, but I do not think peace and friendship between us is too much to ask." She blinked rapidly as she moved her head to avoid his hand. "You promised that—"

"I know what I promised and you have no right to ask more from me. You can't expect to beckon me close and then have me keep my distance," he said harshly. "You can't have it both ways, as you would know if you weren't—" He broke off. "And for God's sake don't *weep*."

"I'm not weeping."

"By God, you are."

"I have something in my eye. You're not being sensible."

"I'm being more sensible than you know," he said with exasperation. "Christ, why the devil is this so important to you?"

She wasn't sure except that it had something to do with that wondrous feeling of *rightness* she had experienced last night. She had never known it before and she would not give it up. She tried to put it into words. "I feel as if I've been closed up inside for a long time. Now I want . . . something else. It will do you no harm to be my friend."

"That's not all you want," he said slowly as he studied her desperate expression. "I don't think you know what you want. But I do and I can't give it to you."

"You could try." She drew a deep breath. "Do you think it's easy for me to ask this of you? It fills me with anger and helplessness and I *hate* that feeling."

She wasn't reaching him. She had to say something that would convince him. Suddenly the words came tumbling out, words she had never meant to say, expressing emotions she had never realized she felt. "I thought all I'd need would be a house but now I know there's something more. I have to have people too. I guess I always knew it but the house was easier, safer. Can't you see? I want what you and Gavin and Angus have, and I don't know if I can find it alone. Sebastian told me I couldn't have it but I will. I *will*." Her hands nervously clenched and unclenched at her sides. "I'm all tight inside. I feel scorched . . . like a desert. Sebastian made me this way and I don't know how to stop. I'm not . . . at ease with anyone."

He smiled ironically. "I've noticed a certain lack of trust in me but you seem to have no problem with Gavin."

"I truly like Gavin but he can't change what I am," she answered, then went on eagerly. "It was different with you last night, though. I really *talked* to you. You made me feel . . ." She stopped. She had sacrificed enough of her pride. If this was not enough, she could give no more.

The only emotion she could identify in the multitude of expressions that flickered across his face was frustration. And there was something else, something darker, more intense. He threw up his hands. "All right, I'll try."

Joy flooded through her. "Truly?"

"My God, you're obstinate."

"It's the only way to keep what one has. If I hadn't fought, you'd have walked away."

"I see." She had the uneasy feeling he saw more than her words had portended. But she must accept this subtle intrusion of apprehension if she was to be fully accepted by him.

"Do I have to make a solemn vow?" he asked with a quizzical lift of his brows.

"Yes, please. Truly?" she persisted.

"Truly." Some of the exasperation left his face. "Satisfied?"

"Yes, that's all I want."

"Is it?" He smiled crookedly. "That's not all I want."

The air between them was suddenly thick and hard to breathe, and Kate could feel the heat burn in her cheeks. She swallowed. "I'm sure you'll get over that once you become accustomed to thinking of me differently."

He didn't answer.

"You'll see." She smiled determinedly and quickly changed the subject. "Where is Gavin?"

"In the kitchen fetching food for the trail."

"I'll go find him and tell him you wish to leave at—"

"In a moment." He moved to stand in front of her and lifted the hood of her cape, then framed her face with a gesture that held a possessive intimacy. He looked down at her, holding her gaze. "This is not a wise thing. I don't know how long I can stand this box you've put me in. All I can promise is that I'll give you warning when I decide to break down the walls."

VIRTUE
by
Jane Feather

"GOLD 5 stars." —*Heartland Critiques*

"An instantaneous attention-grabber. A well-crafted romance with a strong, compelling story and utterly delightful characters." —*Romantic Times*

VIRTUE is the newest regency romance from Jane Feather, four-time winner of Romantic Times's *Reviewer's Choice award, and author of the national bestseller* The Eagle and the Dove.

With a highly sensual style reminiscent of Amanda Quick and Karen Robards, Jane Feather works her bestselling romantic magic with this tale of a strong-willed beauty forced to make her living at the gaming tables, and the arrogant nobleman determined to get the better of her—with passion. The stakes are nothing less than her VIRTUE . . .

What the devil was she doing? Marcus Devlin, the most honorable Marquis of Carrington, absently exchanged his empty champagne glass for a full one as a flunkey passed him. He pushed his shoulders off the wall, straightening to his full height, the better to see across the crowded room to the macao table. She was up to something. Every prickling hair on the nape of his neck told him so.

She was standing behind Charlie's chair, her fan moving in slow sweeps across the lower part of her face. She leaned forward to whisper something in Charlie's ear, and the rich swell of her breasts, the deep shadow of the cleft between them, was uninhibitedly revealed in the décolletage of her evening gown. Charlie looked up at her and smiled, the soft, infatuated smile of puppy love. It wasn't surprising this young cousin had fallen head over heels for Miss Judith Davenport, the marquis reflected. There was hardly a man in Brussels who wasn't stirred by her: a creature of opposites, vibrant, ebullient, sharply intelligent—a woman who in some indefinable fashion challenged a man, put him on his mettle one minute, and yet the next was as appealing as a kitten; a man wanted to pick her up and cuddle her, protect her from the storm . . .

Romantic nonsense! The marquis castigated himself severely for sounding like his cousin and half the young soldiers proudly sporting their regimentals in the salons of Brussels as the world waited for Napoleon to make his move. He'd been watching Judith Davenport weaving her spells for several weeks now, convinced she was an artful minx with a very clear agenda of her own. But for the life of him, he couldn't discover what it was.

His eyes rested on the young man sitting opposite Charlie. Sebastian Davenport held the bank. As beautiful as his sister in his own way, he sprawled in his chair, both clothing and posture radiating a studied carelessness. He was laughing across the table, lightly ruffling the cards in his hands. The mood at the table was lighthearted. It was a mood that always accompanied the Davenports. Presumably one reason why they were so popular . . . and then the marquis saw it.

It was the movement of her fan. There was a pattern to the slow sweeping motion. Sometimes the movement speeded, sometimes it paused, once or twice she snapped the fan closed, then almost immediately began a more vigorous wafting of the delicately painted half moon. There was renewed laughter at the table, and with a lazy sweep of his rake, Sebastian Davenport scooped toward him the pile of vowels and rouleaux in the center of the table.

The marquis walked across the room. As he reached the table, Charlie looked up with a rueful grin. "It's not my night, Marcus."

"It rarely is," Carrington said, taking snuff. "Be careful you don't find yourself in debt." Charlie heard the warning in the advice, for all that his cousin's voice was affably casual. A slight flush tinged the young man's cheekbones and he dropped his eyes to his cards again. Marcus was his guardian and tended to be unsympathetic when Charlie's gaming debts outran his quarterly allowance.

"Do you care to play, Lord Carrington?" Judith Davenport's soft voice spoke at the marquis's shoulder and he turned to look at her. She was smiling, her golden brown eyes luminous, framed in the thickest, curliest eyelashes he had ever seen. However, ten years spent avoiding the frequently blatant blandishments of maidens on the lookout for a rich husband had inured him to the cajolery of a pair of fine eyes.

"No. I suspect it wouldn't be my night either, Miss Davenport. *May* I escort you to the supper room? It must grow tedious, watching my cousin losing hand over fist." He offered a small bow and took her elbow without waiting for a response.

Judith stiffened, feeling the pressure of his hand cupping her bare arm. There was a hardness in his eyes that matched the firmness of his grip, and her scalp contracted as unease shivered across her skin. "On the contrary, my lord, I find the play most entertaining." She gave her arm a covert, experimental tug. His fingers gripped warmly and yet more firmly.

"But I insist, Miss Davenport. You will enjoy a glass of negus."

He had very black eyes and they carried a most unpleasant glitter, as insistent as his tone and words, both of which were drawing a degree of puzzled attention. Judith could see no discreet, graceful escape route. She laughed lightly. "You have convinced me, sir. But I prefer burnt champagne to negus."

"Easily arranged." He drew her arm through his and laid his free hand over hers, resting on his black silk sleeve. Judith felt manacled.

They walked through the card room in a silence that was as uncomfortable as it was pregnant. Had he guessed what was going on? Had he seen anything? How could she have given herself away? Or was it something Sebastian had done, said, looked . . . ? The questions and speculations raced through Judith's brain. She was barely acquainted with Marcus Devlin. He was too sophisticated, too hardheaded to be of use to herself and Sebastian, but she had the distinct sense that he would be an opponent to be reckoned with.

The supper room lay beyond the ballroom, but instead of guiding his companion around the waltzing couples and the ranks of seated chaperones against the wall, Marcus turned aside toward the long French windows opening onto a flagged terrace. A breeze stirred the heavy velvet curtains over an open door.

"I was under the impression we were going to have supper." Judith stopped abruptly.

"No, we're going to take a stroll in the night air," her escort informed her with a bland smile. "Do put one foot in front of the other, my dear ma'am, otherwise our progress might become a little uneven." An unmistakable jerk on her arm drew her forward with a stumble, and Judith rapidly adjusted her gait to match the leisured, purposeful stroll of her companion.

"I don't care for the night air," she hissed through her teeth, keeping a smile on her face. "It's very bad for the constitution and frequently results in the ague or rheumatism."

"Only for those in their dotage," he said, lifting thick black eyebrows. "I would have said you were not a day above twenty-two. Unless you're very skilled with powder and paint?"

He'd pinpointed her age exactly and the sense of being dismayingly out of her depth was intensified. "I'm not quite such an accomplished actress, my lord," she said coldly.

"Are you not?" He held the curtain aside for her and she found herself out on the terrace, lit by flambeaux set in sconces at intervals along the low parapet fronting the sweep of green lawn. "I would have sworn you were as accomplished as any on Drury Lane." The statement was accompanied by a penetrating stare.

Judith rallied her forces and responded to the comment as if it were a humorous compliment. "You're too kind, sir. I confess I've long envied the talent of Mrs. Siddons."

"Oh, you underestimate yourself," he said softly. They had reached the parapet and he stopped under the light of a torch. "You are playing some very pretty theatricals, Miss Davenport, you and your brother."

Judith drew herself up to her full height. It wasn't a

particularly impressive move when compared with her escort's breadth and stature, but it gave her an illusion of hauteur. "I don't know what you're talking about, my lord. It seems you've obliged me to accompany you in order to insult me with vague innuendoes."

"No, there's nothing vague about my accusations," he said. "However insulting they may be. I am assuming my cousin's card play will improve in your absence."

"What are you implying?" The color ebbed in her cheeks, then flooded back in a hot and revealing wave. Hastily she employed her fan in an effort to conceal her agitation.

The marquis caught her wrist and deftly twisted the fan from her hand. "You're most expert with a fan, madam."

"I beg your pardon?" She tried again for a lofty incomprehension, but with increasing lack of conviction.

"Don't continue this charade, Miss Davenport. It benefits neither of us. You and your brother may fleece as many fools as you can find as far as I'm concerned, but you'll leave my cousin alone."

Beneath a Sapphire Sea
by
Jessica Bryan
Rave reviews for Ms. Bryan's novels:

DAWN ON A JADE SEA

"Sensational! Fantastic! There are not enough super-
latives to describe this romantic fantasy. A keeper!"
—*Rendezvous*

"An extraordinary tale of adventure, mystery
and magic." —*Rave Reviews*

ACROSS A WINE-DARK SEA

"Thoroughly absorbing . . . A good read and a promising new author!" —*Nationally bestselling author Anne
McCaffrey*

*Beneath the shimmering, sunlit surface of the ocean there
lives a race of rare and wondrous men and women. They
have walked upon the land, but their true heritage is as
beings of the sea. Now their people face a grave peril. And
one woman holds the key to their survival. . . .*

*A scholar of sea lore, Meredith came to a Greek island to
follow her academic pursuits. But when she encountered
Galen, a proud, determined warrior of the sea, she was
eternally linked with a world far more elusive and mysteri-
ously seductive than her own. For she alone possessed a scroll
that held the secrets of his people.*

*In the following scene, Meredith has just caught Galen
searching for the mysterious scroll. His reaction catches them
both by surprise . . .*

He drew her closer, and Meredith did not resist. To look
away from his face had become impossible. She felt something in him reach out for her, and something in her

answered. It rose up in her like a tide, compelling beyond reason or thought. She lifted her arms and slowly put them around his broad shoulders. He tensed, as if she had startled him, then his whole body seemed to envelop hers as he pulled her against him and lowered his lips to hers.

His arms were like bands of steel, the thud of his heart deep and powerful as a drum, beating in a wild rhythm that echoed the same frantic cadence of Meredith's. His lips seared over hers. His breath was hot in her mouth, and the hard muscles of his bare upper thighs thrust against her lower belly, the bulge between them only lightly concealed by the thin material of his shorts.

Then, as quickly as their lips had come together, they parted.

Galen stared down into Meredith's face, his arms still locked around her slim, strong back. He was deeply shaken, far more than he cared to admit, even to himself. He had been totally focused on probing the landwoman's mind once and for all. Where had the driving urge to kiss her come from, descending on him with a need so strong it had overridden everything else?

He dropped his arms. "That was a mistake," he said, frowning. "I—"

"You're right." Whatever had taken hold of Meredith vanished like the "pop" of a soap bubble, leaving her feeling as though she had fallen headfirst into a cold sea. "It *was* a mistake," she said quickly. "Mine. Now if you'll just get out of here, we can both forget this unfortunate incident ever happened."

She stepped back from him, and Galen saw the anger in her eyes and, held deep below that anger, the hurt. It stung him. None of this was her fault. Whatever forces she exerted upon him, he was convinced she was completely unaware of them. He was equally certain she had no idea of the scroll's significance. To her it was simply an impressive artifact, a rare find that would no doubt gain her great recognition in this folklore profession of hers.

He could not allow that, of course. But the methods he had expected to succeed with her had not worked. He could try again—the very thought of pulling her back into her arms was a seductive one. It played on his senses with heady anticipation, shocking him at how easily this woman could distract him. He would have to find another less physical means of discovering where the scroll was.

"I did not mean it that way," he began in a gentle tone.

Meredith shook her head, refusing to be mollified. She was as taken aback as he by what had happened, and deeply chagrined as well. The fact that she had enjoyed the kiss—No, that was too calm a way of describing it. Galen's mouth had sent rivers of sensations coursing through her, sensations she had not known existed, and that just made the chagrin worse.

"I don't care what you meant," she said in a voice as stiff as her posture. "I've asked you to leave. I don't want to tell you again."

"Meredith, wait." He stepped forward, stopping just short of touching her. "I'm sorry about . . . Please believe my last wish is to offend you. But it does not change the fact that I still want to work with you. And whether you admit it or not, you need me."

"Need you?" Her tone grew frosty. "I don't see how."

"Then you don't see very much," he snapped. He paused to draw in a deep breath, then continued in a placating tone. "Who else can interpret the language on this sheet of paper for you?"

Meredith eyed him. If he was telling the truth, if he really could make sense out on those characters, then, despite the problems he presented, he was an answer to her prayers, to this obsession that would not let her go. She bent and picked up the fallen piece of paper.

"Prove it." She held it out to him. "What does this say?"

He ignored the paper, staring steadily at her. "We will work together, then?"

She frowned as she returned his stare, trying to probe whatever lay behind his handsome face. "Why is it so important to you that we do? I can see why you might think I need you, but what do you get out of this? What do you want, Galen?"

He took the paper from her. *"The season of destruction will soon be upon us and our city,"* he read deliberately, *"but I may have found a way to save some of us, we who were once among the most powerful in the sea. Near the long and narrow island that is but a stone's throw from Crete, the island split by Mother Ocean into two halves . . ."*

He stopped. "It ends there." His voice was low and fierce, as fierce as his gaze, which seemed to reach out to grip her. "Are you satisfied now? Or do you require still more proof?"

TEMPTING EDEN
by
Maureen Reynolds

author of SMOKE EYES

"Ms. Reynolds blends steamy sensuality with
marvelous lovers. . . . delightful."
—*Romantic Times on SMOKE EYES*

*Eden Victoria Lindsay knew it was foolish to break into the
home of one of New York's most famous—and reclusive—
private investigators. Now she had fifteen minutes to convince him that he shouldn't have her thrown in prison.*

*Shane O'Connor hardly knew what to make of the flaxen-
haired aristocrat who'd scaled the wall of his Long Island
mansion—except that she was in more danger than she
suspected. In his line of work, trusting the wrong woman
could get a man killed, but Shane is about to himself get
taken in by this alluring and unconventional beauty. . . .*

"She scaled the wall, sir," said Simon, Shane's stern
butler.

Eden rolled her eyes. "Yes—yes, I did! And I'd do it
again—a hundred times. How else could I reach the
impossible *inaccessible* Mr. O'Connor?"

He watched her with a quiet intensity but it was Simon
who answered, "If one wishes to speak with Mr. O'Connor, a meeting is usually arranged through the *proper*
channels."

Honestly, Eden thought, the English aristocracy did
not look down their noses half so well as these two!

O'Connor stepped gracefully out of the light and his

gaze, falling upon her, was like the steel of gunmetal. He leaned casually against the wall—his weight on one hip, his hands in his trousers pockets—and he studied her with half-veiled eyes.

"Have you informed the . . . ah . . . *lady*, Simon, what type of reception our unexpected guests might anticipate? Especially," he added in a deceptively soft tone, "those who scale the estate walls, and . . . er . . . shed their clothing?"

Eden stiffened, her face hot with color; he'd made it sound as if it were *commonplace* for women to scale his wall and undress.

Simon replied, "Ah, no, sir. In the melee, that particular formality slipped my mind."

"Do you suppose we should strip her first, or just torture her?"

"*What?*"

"Or would you rather we just arrest you, madame?"

"Sir, with your attitude it is a wonder you have a practice at all!"

"It is a wonder," he drawled coldly, "that you are still alive, madame. You're a damn fool to risk your neck as you did. Men have been shot merely for attempting it, and I'm amazed you weren't killed yourself."

Eden brightened. "Then I am to be commended, am I not? Congratulate me, sir, for accomplishing such a feat!"

Shane stared at her as if she were daft.

"And for my prowess you should be more than willing to give me your time. Please, just listen to my story! I promise I will pay you handsomely for your time!"

As her eyes met his, Eden began to feel hope seep from her. At her impassioned plea there was no softening in his chiseled features, or in his stony gaze. In a final attempt she gave him her most imploring look, and then instantly regretted it, for the light in his eyes suddenly burned brighter. It was as if he knew her game.

"State your business," O'Connor bit out.

"I need you to find my twin brother."

Shane frowned. "You have a twin?"

"Yes I do."

God help the world, he thought.

He leaned to crush out his cheroot, his gaze watching

her with a burning, probing intensity. "*Why* do you need me to find your twin?"

"Because he's missing, of course," she said in a mildly exasperated voice.

Shane brought his thumb and forefinger up to knead the bridge of his nose. "*Why*, do you need me to find him? *Why* do you think he is missing, and not on some drunken spree entertaining the . . . uh . . . 'ladies'?"

"Well, Mr. O'Connor, that's very astute of you—excuse me, do you have a headache, sir?"

"Not yet."

Eden hurried on. "Actually I might agree with you that Philip could be on a drunken spree, but the circumstances surrounding his disappearance don't match that observation."

Shane lifted a brow.

"You see, Philip *does* spend a good deal of time in the brothels, and there are three in particular that he frequents. But the madames of all of them told me they haven't seen him for several days."

Shane gave her a strange look. "You went into a brothel?"

"No. I went into *three*. And Philip wasn't in any of them." She thought she caught the tiniest flicker of amusement in his silver eyes, then quickly dismissed the notion. Unlikely the man had a drop of mirth in him.

"What do you mean by 'the circumstances matching the observation'?"

Eden suddenly realized she had not produced a shred of evidence. "Please turn around and look away from me Mr. O'Connor."

"Like hell."

Though her heart thudded hard, Eden smiled radiantly. "But you must! You have to!"

"I don't *have* to do anything I don't damn well please, madame."

"Please, Mr. O'Connor." Her tearing eyes betrayed her guise of confidence. "I-I brought some evidence I think might help you with the case—that is if you take it. But it's—I had to carry it under my skirt. Please," she begged softly.

Faintly amused, Shane shifted his gaze out toward the bay. Out of the corner of his eye he saw her twirl around, hoist her layers of petticoats to her waist, and fumble with something.

She turned around again, and with a dramatic flair that was completely artless, she opened the chamois bag she had tied to the waistband of her pantalets. She grabbed his hand and plopped a huge, uncut diamond into the center of his palm. Then she took hold of his other hand and plunked down another stone—an extraordinary grass-green emerald as large as the enormous diamond.

"Where," he asked in a hard drawl, "did you get these?"

"That," Eden said, "is what I've come to tell you."

OFFICIAL RULES

To enter the sweepstakes below carefully follow all instructions found elsewhere in this offer.

The **Winners Classic** will award prizes with the following approximate maximum values: 1 Grand Prize: $26,500 (or $25,000 cash alternate); 1 First Prize: $3,000; 5 Second Prizes: $400 each; 35 Third Prizes: $100 each; 1,000 Fourth Prizes: $7.50 each. Total maximum retail value of Winners Classic Sweepstakes is $42,500. Some presentations of this sweepstakes may contain individual entry numbers corresponding to one or more of the aforementioned prize levels. To determine the Winners, individual entry numbers will first be compared with the winning numbers preselected by computer. For winning numbers not returned, prizes will be awarded in random drawings from among all eligible entries received. Prize choices may be offered at various levels. If a winner chooses an automobile prize, all license and registration fees, taxes, destination charges and, other expenses not offered herein are the responsibility of the winner. If a winner chooses a trip, travel must be complete within one year from the time the prize is awarded. Minors must be accompanied by an adult. Travel companion(s) must also sign release of liability. Trips are subject to space and departure availability. Certain black-out dates may apply.

The following applies to the sweepstakes named above:

No purchase necessary. You can also enter the sweepstakes by sending your name and address to: P.O. Box 508, Gibbstown, N.J. 08027. Mail each entry separately. Sweepstakes begins 6/1/93. Entries must be received by 12/30/94. Not responsible for lost, late, damaged, misdirected, illegible or postage due mail. Mechanically reproduced entries are not eligible. All entries become property of the sponsor and will not be returned.

Prize Selection/Validations: Selection of winners will be conducted no later than 5:00 PM on January 28, 1995, by an independent judging organization whose decisions are final. Random drawings will be held at 1211 Avenue of the Americas, New York, N.Y. 10036. Entrants need not be present to win. Odds of winning are determined by total number of entries received. Circulation of this sweepstakes is estimated not to exceed 200 million. All prizes are guaranteed to be awarded and delivered to winners. Winners will be notified by mail and may be required to complete an affidavit of eligibility and release of liability which must be returned within 14 days of date on notification or alternate winners will be selected in a random drawing. Any prize notification letter or any prize returned to a participating sponsor, Bantam Doubleday Dell Publishing Group, Inc., its participating divisions or subsidiaries, or the independent judging organization as undeliverable will be awarded to an alternate winner. Prizes are not transferable. No substitution for prizes except as offered or as may be necessary due to unavailability, in which case a prize of equal or greater value will be awarded. Prizes will be awarded approximately 90 days after the drawing. All taxes are the sole responsibility of the winners. Entry constitutes permission (except where prohibited by law) to use winners' names, hometowns, and likenesses for publicity purposes without further or other compensation. Prizes won by minors will be awarded in the name of parent or legal guardian.

Participation: Sweepstakes open to residents of the United States and Canada, except for the province of Quebec. Sweepstakes sponsored by Bantam Doubleday Dell Publishing Group, Inc., (BDD), 1540 Broadway, New York, NY 10036. Versions of this sweepstakes with different graphics and prize choices will be offered in conjunction with various solicitations or promotions by different subsidiaries and divisions of BDD. Where applicable, winners will have their choice of any prize offered at level won. Employees of BDD, its divisions, subsidiaries, advertising agencies, independent judging organization, and their immediate family members are not eligible.

Canadian residents, in order to win, must first correctly answer a time limited arithmetical skill testing question. Void in Puerto Rico, Quebec and wherever prohibited or restricted by law. Subject to all federal, state, local and provincial laws and regulations. For a list of major prize winners (available after 1/29/95): send a self-addressed, stamped envelope entirely separate from your entry to: Sweepstakes Winners, P.O. Box 517, Gibbstown, NJ 08027. Requests must be received by 12/30/94. DO NOT SEND ANY OTHER CORRESPONDENCE TO THIS P.O. BOX.